WHAT MAKES an ALIEN a DAD?

My Holiday Tails

Marina Simcoe

To my Captain,

who is the best dad ever

What Makes an Alien a Dad?

Chapter 1

Maya

"*P*ooh *Bear,*
I know it sucks, but I hope you'll understand. You're a smart, strong girl. That's why I loved you all these years..."

Loved?

Past tense?

My heart stuttered, and it took a moment for it to restart. Even then, it didn't seem to work all that well; my feet and hands went cold, blood rushing away from them.

What was this letter from Walter, my boyfriend, practically my fiancé, supposed to mean?

I was afraid to continue reading, but my eyes ran down the glowing dark-blue lines of text on the opaque screen of the tablet I'd received for my personal use upon arrival to the planet Neron five months ago.

"The truth is, these ten months have been hard..."

No one expected them to be easy. We'd talked about it a lot before I left Earth. Both Walter and I knew that my long absence might be challenging for our relationship. But it'd been a mutual decision.

I'd shared everything with Walter, including every piece of communication I'd received from Neron back then. My medical tests turned out to be the most promising out of hundreds of others, deeming my uterus the best place on Earth for the development of a Voranian baby.

Walter and I decided together that I should participate in the experimental study as the first human surrogate to implant the embryo of anonymous donors from the country of Voran located on Planet Neron.

For us, it'd be a great opportunity to earn the money Walter needed to open his store. And for Voranians, it offered new opportunities to become parents for the human-Voranian couples on Neron.

Historically, there were far more boys than girls born in Voran. It resulted in a ratio of about one woman to nine or ten men. In addition to their own families, Voranian women often used artificial insemination to help men other than their husbands to start a family as single fathers.

With the creation of the Earth-Neron Liaison Committee several years ago, a marriage agreement was signed. Human women could apply to become wives of Voranian men. Several happy marriages had formed since.

However, humans could not reproduce with Voranians. Our species turned out to be biologically incompatible for procreation.

The goal of the study I'd been selected for was to give human wives of Voranian men the chance to carry the babies of their husbands on their own with the help of a Voranian egg donor. If successful, the results of the studies would benefit everyone.

For the Voranian women, it meant they would have to go through fewer pregnancies. The embryos created with donor eggs and the sperm of a Voranian man married to a human woman would be implanted directly into his wife, allowing her to carry the pregnancy to term.

A win-win situation.

Unfortunately, after months or even years of extensive tests and research, I'd been deemed the only suitable human subject so far.

Voranians had been ecstatic to get their hands on me and my uterus. They couldn't force me to participate in the study, of course, but they'd made their offer as enticing as possible. I'd gotten an all-expense-paid trip to Voran, including the spaceship travel, accommodation, and whatever else I needed, provided it was approved by the head of the study, Professor Thormus. I'd also received a large payment before I'd even boarded the spaceship, and I had been promised five times as much upon the completion of the study.

This was supposed to be our new start, Walter's and mine. Nineteen to twenty months spent apart didn't seem too bad, considering we'd been together since we were sixteen—ten years now. We'd talked about getting married as soon as I got back to Earth, which would be only nine more months, including the five-month-long trip back.

The long-distance relationship hadn't been easy. We mostly communicated by written messages. Sending occasional videos was also allowed by my contract. We'd managed just fine. The study was more than half-way through already.

But now, this letter from Walter came...

"I feel like my life has been put on hold. I have a girlfriend who isn't here. Technically, I'm in a relationship, but I have to do everything alone. I feel out of place at both single and couple events. It sucks..."

Well, it sucked for me, too. But we were in it together. Except that I also had to go through our separation while carrying an alien fetus in my belly.

"Anyway, I hope you understand, Pooh Bear. I'm sorry, but I just can't go on like this..."

What?

What was that supposed to mean?

I got up from the small table on the rooftop terrace of the hospital building in Voran that had been my home since my arrival on Neron. My nose started to prickle from the inside, and my vision blurred. I blinked to clear the haze, but it barely helped.

The text on the tablet screen appeared to swim.

"I've been trying to figure out the best way to tell you, but it is what it is. I want to be single, Maya. Properly single, without having a girlfriend out there among the stars somewhere..."

A sob bubbled up my throat, and I threw a hand over my mouth.

The beautiful rooftop gardens weren't crowded, but there were people around. A few hospital technicians in white coveralls strolled along the mosaic stone paths. A couple were sitting on a bench two tables away from me, having lunch.

I tried to hide my face from view, hiding behind my dark, long hair.

Ten years... I'd been with Walter for ten years, and all it took for our relationship to fall apart was a few months spent away from each other.

"I hate to hurt you, Pooh Bear, but I have to be completely honest here. Maybe I just don't love you enough to go ahead with this commitment. Maybe I grew to love my single life too much. I never really had a chance to be single before..."

My next breath came rough and coarse. I hurried along the path. My chest tightened. Tears burned behind my eyelids, but I couldn't let them out in public.

How could he?

How could he do this to me when I'm millions of miles away from home? I was the only human in this entire hospital. As part of the study, I wasn't allowed to leave, to socialize, or to make friends with anyone outside of the premises.

Walter was my main connection to the outside world. And now, he was leaving me...

I sniffled, desperately trying to hold back my tears.

"Are you alright?" one of the technicians asked sympathetically while passing by.

His kindness undid me.

I nodded, hiding behind my hair, and almost sprinted around the tall hedge toward the exit. But I didn't make it. Tears ran down my face in a torrential stream. My knees gave out.

Two Voranian nurses appeared up ahead. The last thing I wanted was to cause a scene. I scrambled off the path and under the nearest tree. Crouching, I climbed into a bush with big yellow flowers and let the tears flow.

I felt so alone, like I was the only person in the entire Universe.

Chapter 2

Kear

On the way from the lab to his office, Kear made a detour to grab a lunch tray from the small café in the gardens on the roof of the hospital building.

Of course, he could have sent a drone to pick it up instead of walking three floors up only to go four floors down right after, but excitement buzzed through him, spurring him to move. The bounce in his step was so pronounced, he was practically dancing on his hooves.

On his way to the café, he went over the latest charts on his tablet. It looked good. Everything looked so fucking good, it was scary. Concerns could spring up unexpectedly with any pregnancy. But when it was the one-of-a-kind pregnancy in the entire Universe, everything was a risk.

The last five months had been the most intense in his life, which was significant, considering his life before hadn't always been easy, either. Yet this study proved more challenging than anything he'd done before.

Thankfully, the hard work seemed to be paying off. The subject's hormone levels were great. Her health seemed fine. The fetus's measurements were on the lower end of the scale but still within normal range. All organs looked perfect.

For the first time ever, a Voranian fetus was thriving in a human womb. It was a huge achievement. He couldn't wait to present his findings at the assembly this weekend. He could already imagine the envious looks on the faces of Hezer and Egus.

The three of them graduated from the academy together. Kear had been in the top of his class, but he'd taken a break right after to serve as a field doctor during the last two years of the war with the *fescods,* the semi-intelligent blob-like creatures that had taken over the nearby planet Tragul before invading the Voranian planet Neron. It had been the most brutal war in this part of the galaxy.

He'd learned a lot during his years on the battlefield and gained skills he would not have been able to gain anywhere else—like working without modern medical equipment, treating wounds with medicine sourced from local plants and animals, or thinking fast and taking risks that saved lives. It'd been a valuable experience, but it had set him back academically.

When he resumed his studies and his research work after the war, he had to catch up. Many of his colleagues had advanced far beyond him.

He got lucky, incredibly lucky, to stumble upon the breakthrough before anyone else. Since he was the one who'd found the subject with the best compatibility score, he had been appointed as the Head of Research during the most important study in the reproductive field yet.

Kear was only thirty-four—a ridiculously young age in the science world. Everything he'd achieved since his lucky break was through hard work, learning, and determination. Yet he found himself constantly having to defend his accomplishments in front of his much older and more experienced colleagues.

Well, at the assembly this weekend, he'd prove that the respect and honor he'd received from the nation was well earned on his part. The human subject of his study—

A strangled sob coming from the bushes beside the stone path made him pause. Tearing his attention away from his tablet screen, he lifted his head.

Another sob came—a squeaky, pitiful sound, followed by a sniffle. It appeared someone was crying. Only he couldn't see anyone around.

Not that he knew what to do with a crying person, even if he saw them. The best he could think of would be getting a drone for assistance.

He lifted his tablet again, intending to call a hospital drone, when movement caught his eye. A foot in a white hospital shoe shifted on the ground, quickly disappearing under the nearest bush.

Voranians had hooves and wore no shoes. To his knowledge, there was currently only one pair of feet in this entire hospital. And it belonged to his study subject.

If she was the one crying, it was a problem, and it concerned him directly.

He lowered his tablet, staring at the dirt under the bush where the foot had just been. Another sob came from behind the flowers. This one was barely audible as she must've noticed him and covered her mouth with her hands, not wanting him to hear her crying.

Fuck, he didn't want to hear it either. If there was one thing that made him feel uncomfortably helpless, it was a crying woman. He had no idea what to do and wished he could just pretend he heard nothing, get his food, and eat it in peace in his office, like he'd intended.

But the human was crying. Which meant she was in distress. Which in turn meant her mental wellbeing was in jeopardy. Her physical wellbeing might also be at risk, and so were his perfect charts he was about to present at the biggest assembly in his field.

He couldn't let a drone handle this.

"Um..." He cleared his throat, speaking to the bush. "Madam..."

What was her name again? In all the research documents, she was referred to only by the subject number. Of course, he'd personally signed her immigration papers. He'd seen her full name listed there. But what was it? As great as his memory was at retaining large strings of research data, any irrelevant information didn't stay there for long.

"Madam." He decided to omit the name for now. "May I inquire what has caused your distress?"

The bush remained quiet; even the sobbing had ceased. Well, there was not much left to do. Crouching down, he set aside his tablet and parted the flower-covered branches.

She sat on the ground, hugging her knees as closely as her protruding belly allowed. The white cap she had worn during the physical exam that morning was gone. Her thick black hair was spread over her shoulders, with a few long tresses hanging over her face. Her dark eyes glistened as she glared at him through her thick, glossy strands.

"I'm fine."

She obviously lied. She looked the opposite of fine. The skin around her eyes was puffy. Her cheeks were flushed, making her appear feverish. Tears streaked her face.

Unease crawled up Kear's spine, urging him to flee. He felt way out of his element here. He'd much rather face a raging *fescod*. At least then, he'd know what to do. But he couldn't leave her like this. Her pulse must be racing. Her blood pressure was likely elevated. Neither would look good on his daily report charts.

"Can I take you to your apartment?" he asked.

Actually, he should take her back to the lab and take an entirely new set of data. Just to make sure nothing horrible was threatening his study subject.

Worry wormed into his chest.

"Are you hurt? Any cramping? Bleeding?"

His heart thumped in his chest at the last word. Risk factors could spring up during any pregnancy. And this one was so unique, even he didn't know exactly what to expect.

Misery eased from her expression. She made a visible effort to collect herself.

"No. Sorry, Professor Thormus. I didn't mean to scare you. I'm well. Just..." She sniffed again, glancing aside. "Just some things from back home... Nothing to worry about."

He noticed a tablet on the ground next to her. Irritation stirred in him. He had considered forbidding her all outside communications for the duration of the study, but Representative Alcus Hecear from the Voranian branch of the Liaison Committee convinced him that keeping in touch with the subject's loved ones would be good for her mental health.

Now, he could punch himself for agreeing with that. Any communication carried the risk of receiving bad news, and bad news never improved anyone's wellbeing.

"You can go, Professor Thormus." She waved at him. "I'll be fine. Promise."

The fact that she knew his name made him feel guilty about having forgotten hers. But then again, this clinic bore his name. It was on the signs on every floor and all official documentation. It made it much easier to remember.

Hers, on the other hand...

"Listen, Madam... Um."

She wiped the tears off her cheeks with the end of the hospital robe she was wearing over the examination gown. "Just Maya."

"Pardon me?"

"You can just call me Maya. It's my first name. You don't have to say Madam Gupta all the time."

He'd never said either. But at least now he had her name.

Maya.

It was short enough to remember.

She kept rubbing at her cheeks with her robe, sitting in the dirt of the flowerbed. He cringed at the thought of the germs she must've picked up by crawling around. Producing a pack of sanitizing wipes from his pocket, he handed her one.

"Here. It's gentle enough to use on your face." He pulled out another one. "And this one is for your hands."

"Thanks." She took the wipes, cleaned her face and hands, then blew her nose.

With all those tears running for who knew how long, she must be dehydrated. She likely hadn't had lunch yet either if she'd been sitting here since her morning exam.

"When was the last time you ate?"

She balled up the wipes and stuffed them into the pocket of her robe.

"I'm not hungry."

Hunger had nothing to do with it. She required a steady flow of nutrition to ensure an optimal environment for the fetus. Skipping meals was unacceptable and against the rules outlined in the contract.

"Come. I'll get you lunch." He climbed to his hooves.

There was a smudge on the left pant leg of his coverall. The dirt from the flower bed must have gotten on it somehow, despite his best efforts to avoid it. He winced at the sight of the dark-brown stain on the crisp white fabric. But there were infinitely more stains on the human's clothes. He had to get her out of those bushes.

"Come on." He offered her a hand.

"I'd rather stay here," she said softly. Her bottom lip trembled. She looked utterly miserable once again.

He rubbed his forehead, trying to figure out what to do about this situation.

"Should I call Alcus Hecear?"

Representative Alcus Hecear was everything Kear was not—smiling, diplomatic, tactful, a people person in every way. As the Head of the Liaison Committee, Alcus was involved in dealing with any problems occurring in human-Voranian relationships. Humans loved him. Voranians respected him. He would know how to coax Maya out of this bush.

Kear turned on his tablet, ready to request Alcus's contact.

"No. Don't." She sighed. "I don't want to make a scene. It's not a big deal." Getting on all fours, she finally crawled out of the bushes, then retrieved her tablet. "I'll just go back to my apartment now."

He couldn't let her out of his sight, not while she looked so miserable, like an *ulto* pup pulled out of water.

"Why don't you have lunch with me?" He blinked in shock at his own proposition.

He always ate alone, unless it couldn't be helped, like during formal meetings or official functions. He certainly didn't remember ever inviting anyone to share a meal before. But he couldn't trust his subject to eat something nutritious if he allowed her to return to her apartment on her own. He suspected she'd just cry again and miss lunch completely. It was best to feed her where he could supervise her food intake.

"What's your favorite Voranian food?" he asked. "Today, I'll allow you to have whatever you like on top of your pre-planned meal."

"Really?" Her smile was sad and rather pitiful, but it was so much better than tears. "Anything I like? Even if it's not on the list of approved stuff?"

He hesitated. The list was there for a reason. He'd personally compiled it, matching human ingredients to Voranian ones to ensure a proper mix of nutrients for her.

"Is there something you'd like outside of that list?" he asked tentatively.

"*Ice cream,*" she replied way too quickly. She'd clearly had it in mind for some time now. "Or whatever closest substitute you have for it in Voran. Frozen cream with sugar, chocolate, and caramel sauce."

His translator implant fired off the Voranian substitutes of the ingredients she'd listed. None of them were on the list of the approved foods, because all of them would wreak havoc on her system.

He stared at her in horror. The woman was a menace to herself.

"How about some frozen cultured milk with fruit juice and berries instead?" he suggested. She made a face, and he added quickly, "That's as close a substitute as you'll get in my clinic."

She dropped her shoulders and silently followed him to the order counter of the rooftop café as if he were leading her to an execution.

Why did it bother him so much to see her upset?

"Fine." He pinched the bridge of his nose. "I'll let them sweeten it."

She perked up, glancing at the order screen from around his bicep. "You'll add sugar?"

Absolutely not.

"A tree nectar from the planet Tragul," he named a much healthier alternative to the sweetener that she referred to. "It contains traces of several useful nutrients, at least."

"But what does it taste like?"

"Like flowers. You'll like it."

Chapter 3

Maya

Of all the people in the Universe, it was Professor Thormus who had to find me while I was having a meltdown.

The man was the least approachable person I'd ever met. He'd been examining me almost daily for the past five months, but we'd hardly exchanged a handful of words until today. It always felt like being examined by a robot. He'd insert a probe into my vagina, and it'd be like I wasn't even there. Which was perfect and exactly what I expected from a man who wasn't my boyfriend looking at my private parts.

But now, my vagina seemed to be the only thing that connected us, which didn't give us much material for small talk.

At the thought of my boyfriend, Walter's letter came to mind again, and my eyes watered despite my best efforts.

"Here is your dessert." Professor Thormus shoved a frosted glass with pink ice milk my way. Peering at me, he appeared even more uncomfortable at the sign of impending tears. "You know what? Just drink it now, before lunch. It's fine, as a one-time exception."

I grabbed the glass and took a long drink of the fruity, mildly sweet concoction. It was good and refreshing. The best thing I'd tasted since boarding the spaceship to Neron, not counting the cupcakes I'd smuggled into my apartment yesterday, unbeknownst to the professor.

I studied him over the rim of my glass. He looked worried, his bushy eyebrows close together, his purple eyes glistening intently from under them. How had I not noticed before that his eyes were such a pretty color?

Voranians were gray from head to toe, um...head to *hoof*. But their eyes came in all possible colors, from lime green to purple and even bright red.

Typical for his species, the professor had charcoal-gray skin. Most parts of him not covered by his crisp, white lab coverall sported thick, gray fur. It was neatly trimmed and styled on his head between his two long polished horns and along his strong jawline. On his face, the fur was so short, it was barely noticeable, lying flat against his nose and prominent cheekbones. The fur thinned on the back of his hands, with his palms left completely furless.

His eyes stood out on his dark-gray face like two bright gems. It was unexpectedly pretty for a man like him.

He flinched under my scrutiny, and I quickly dropped my gaze to my drink, afraid I'd stared at him for too long.

The café drone delivered the rest of our order, two trays with sixteen small indentations, each holding a different piece of food. I liked that about Voranian meals. They never contained just one thing. Voranians preferred variety. Each small portion had its own unique flavor, which made for an exciting experience for my taste buds.

The only problem was that my meal plan didn't include much variety. Every single tray I'd had lately contained pretty much the same variation of wholesome, nutritious but oh-so-boring items.

I noted with surprise that the professor's tray held very much the same stuff as mine. It was weird that he would limit himself like this. After all, *he* wasn't pregnant with the planet's most important fetus and could eat anything he liked.

"So, um..." He poked with a narrow utensil at the piece of lean meat in one of the indentations on his tray. "How do you find living in Voran?"

He looked so stiff, his muscles must be cramping. Small talk clearly wasn't the professor's forte. It wasn't mine, either. I would prefer to eat alone, back in my apartment. But since he attempted to be social for my sake, I could do the same.

"It's good," I said politely.

He nodded.

We proceeded to eat in silence. In an awkward silence, I might add. Maybe I should just take the food to my apartment and let him go on with his day? He must be busy, with a ton of stuff to do. Unlike me, who had nothing to do at all.

I wasn't allowed to leave the hospital building, and as huge as the building was, there wasn't that much to explore. After wandering its halls for five months now, I pretty much knew every nook and cranny of this seventy-six story high-rise. Despite that many floors, all of them looked very much the same.

Lately, I mostly just sat in my apartment, watched Voranian movies, and ate the healthy rations they served me.

Last week, however, I met a nurse on the twenty-seventh floor. She didn't belong to Professor Thormus's clinic and didn't work for him. Unaware of my super strict meal plan, she told me about the place called Earth Girl's Desserts. Apparently, that was a bakery owned by the first human woman who'd married a Voranian man. She baked cupcakes from local ingredients but managed to make them taste just like those back on Earth. At least that was what the nurse had said.

Yesterday, the nurse brought me a box of four cupcakes from that bakery. I immediately gobbled up one, and it was divine, like the taste of home with heavenly sweetness.

All I really wanted right now was to go back to my apartment, eat the rest of the cupcakes, and cry to my heart's content.

But Professor Thormus took some time from his busy schedule to have lunch with me. The least I could do was to spare a few minutes from my day of doing nothing and have lunch with him.

I racked my brain for a topic to keep the conversation afloat. It was hard, since I knew absolutely nothing about him, even though I saw him almost daily and had a ton of his probes inside my body on a regular basis.

"What made you choose a career in the reproductive field, Professor?" And now I sounded like I was interviewing him for a local newspaper.

Fortunately, his face lit up at the question. Clearly, that was the subject he was very comfortable with.

"Medical field was identified as predominant on my aptitude test, along with general science," he said.

From the movies, I knew Voranian babies went through aptitude tests from the day they were born. They spent their childhood in the academy matched with their born abilities, following an individual development plan tailored specifically for them.

"It wasn't surprising," the professor continued, "since my father was a renowned surgeon. He's retired now, but he'd worked most of his life in this very hospital."

"I didn't know that. Is that why you opened your clinic here, too?"

"Yes." He nodded, swaying his long horns. "I never even considered any other location. As for my choice of reproductive field..." He twisted the utensil between his long fingers, looking contemplative. "I made this choice during my two years as the field doctor on Tragul."

"You've been to war?"

From watching Voranian television, I'd learned all about the twenty-year-long war waged between Ravils, a nation on the planet Tragul, and the *fescods*, the blob-shaped creatures governed by a central mind.

At some point, *fescods* invaded Neron, too, forcing Voran to fight on their own territory. Earth had sent a unit of specialized armored soldiers as well, helping the two planets to finally defeat the *fescods* and end the long, bloody war.

Never in a million years would I have imagined this neat, distant, always so well put-together professor fighting in the mud and grime of the battlefields.

"I spent only two years at war before it ended. But I hope my service contributed to our ultimate victory," he said.

"Of course it did." I nodded enthusiastically. "I saw a very good documentary on it. Although the end of the war was brought on by one action, every bit before that counted in stopping those things from causing more damage and devastation."

He tilted his head, giving me a curious look. He clearly didn't expect me to be familiar with the Voranian history. But what else did I have to do other than watch shows and movies? I couldn't even read unless the book was narrated to me, since translator implants only worked with sound, not visual language.

"It was during those two years on Tragul," he said, "that I decided to fully commit to the reproductive area of my work."

"Why?"

He rubbed his jaw under his short beard.

"I saw more deaths in the field hospital than I'd ever seen in my entire life prior. We did our best. But many lives were lost despite our efforts. Before I even returned to Neron, I knew I wanted to help bring new life into this world."

His reasoning sounded profound.

"I didn't expect that," I blurted out.

He arched an eyebrow. "You didn't?"

"No. I'm sorry, I..."

"What did you think was my reason for doing what I do?"

"Oh, I don't know. Money maybe? Accolades? Fame?"

He just didn't strike me as an emotional type, not by any stretch of imagination. I'd assumed a pragmatic person like him would be motivated mostly by practical things.

"Money is good to have," he agreed. "The importance of this work is high for our country, therefore this study is very well funded. Accolades are great both for my ego and reputation." He smiled. "But fame...

Fame I could certainly do without. People are starting to recognize me in public, and it's becoming rather bothersome."

"I suppose it is."

"They would bother you, too, out there. That's one of the reasons why I put the clause into our contract about not leaving the hospital premises during the study. You don't need that kind of attention."

"Oh, *you* put it in? Does it mean you're the one who could take it out, too?"

He blinked at me. "Why would I do that?"

"It'd be nice to see Voran City, other than through the glass." I gestured at the giant dome that covered the entire roof top of the building.

The nearly six-month-long Voranian winter had ended. As was typical for this planet, the change of the season lasted only a week. The snow had already melted, and the sun was shining brightly. I wouldn't even mind some public attention if it meant I could go outside for a little while.

"This building has everything a person needs," the professor stated firmly, crushing my hopes of ever getting out of here while under his control.

It was ironic how much I wished to get some fresh air, considering I was a homebody by nature. But it seemed even an introvert like me could reach a limit of indoor time after five months in the hospital and five on the spaceship before that.

"By contract," he added. "You're allowed to stay in Voran up to a month after the completion of the study. You can do whatever you wish then."

"Right. I guess I'll wait." I mashed a cube of a steamed vegetable with my utensil, then scooped it up and shoved it into my mouth.

The conversation fizzled out again, and this time the professor was the one to attempt to revive it.

"Tell me why you decided to participate in our study, Maya."

I smiled somewhat sheepishly. "I wish I could say something poignant and profound, too, Professor, but my main motivation was money."

He paused his gaze on me. "Did you struggle financially?"

Who didn't? Even those who appeared well-off always seemed to wish for more money, no matter how much they had.

"Well, I wasn't living on the street or starving, but Walt—" I cut myself off, unwilling to say his name out loud, lest I break down sobbing again. I cleared my throat before continuing. "We wanted to open a sporting goods store. One that would sell everything from hiking gear to exercise equipment. It required a substantial capital investment."

"And that was enough for you to commit to an extensive and invasive study like this one? To leave your home planet and part from your loved ones? Every aspect of your current life is strictly regulated."

"Yeah, the contract rules are rather strict." I didn't realize he was behind them all. Somehow, I'd imagined the design of this study was a result of planning by a large group of people, possibly of several organizations, including the government. I never thought one man held this much power over me. "But it wasn't *just* money, of course. The opportunity to experience life on another planet was exciting. The study seemed important, too."

He shifted eagerly. "This study is of the utmost importance, Maya. If all goes as well as it has been so far—and I will do everything to ensure it does—the results will improve the lives of all Voranian families. Our women have been bearing the enormous responsibility of maintaining our population growth. Because of their relatively low numbers, they each have to go through multiple pregnancies, carrying not only the children of their husbands but also of other men wishing to become fathers. The bodies of Voranian women are well equipped for multiples, and they have been coping well. But they are looking forward to the opportunity to spend less time pregnant."

"I don't blame them."

"Why?" He looked concerned again. "Is pregnancy causing you trouble?"

"No. I feel fine. You're way too jumpy, Professor," I teased with a light smile.

"A lot of hope is hinging on your wellbeing, Maya."

"I know. But I really do feel fine, everything considered. I just meant that growing another person in your body does take its toll. I understand Voranian women's desire to have fewer pregnancies. Especially, since almost all of theirs are of multiples."

Curiosity shone in his pretty violet eyes. "What do you think about being in the study? How do you like being a part of it?"

"Well, this is my first time being pregnant, but I kind of knew what to expect when I signed up. My sister-in-law, the wife of one of my brothers, has been a surrogate twice."

"Why did she do it?"

"To help couples who couldn't have a baby on their own and to earn some money while my brother was working overseas. I talked to her a lot before coming here. She gave me a ton of good advice about being a surrogate."

"I didn't know you'd completed some preliminary research on your own." He looked impressed.

"I'd hardly call it research." I waved a hand. "But yes, it definitely helped me prepare for what to expect, in addition to the counseling provided by the Liaison Committee."

He seemed pleased with my answers. And I was glad to have something to think about that didn't involve Walter's letter. The news from that letter was hanging over me like a black cloud, but I did my best to ignore it, studying the Voranian professor instead.

Most of my previous encounters with Professor Thormus had been with me lying on the examination table, his attention focused mostly on my lower body. I hadn't had a chance to interact with him face to face before.

He ate unhurriedly, picking up the food with his utensil in measured movements. I couldn't tell whether he liked any of the pieces better than others. He spent an equal amount of time chewing each of them, and his expression remained the same.

The sleeve of his coverall stretched over his bicep as he lifted the utensil to his mouth. I never paid much attention to his body before, but the professor seemed to pack some serious muscles into his lab clothes. He also appeared younger than I'd thought. His face and hands had hardly any lines yet.

"What did you think of the food?" He asked, gesturing with his fork at my empty tray.

"It's boring, like always," I said without thinking, then added quickly. "But nutritious, I guess."

"Very nutritious," he said with emphasis. "And the dessert? Do you like it?"

I took another sip of the drink.

"The dessert is a welcome change." I licked my lips, savoring the taste of something different for once.

His tablet dinged with a notification. He glanced at it but didn't pick it up.

"Do you need to go?" I asked.

Of course he did. He was a medical professor, the supervisor of an extensive study, and the owner of a prestigious medical clinic. He must be busy up to his horns. And here I was, wasting his time.

"It can wait," he assured me.

But I finished my drink quickly.

"We can go." I got up from the table. "Thank you so much for having lunch with me. It's not every day I have company."

I ended up forcing my company on other people lately, like I did with that nurse from the twenty-seventh floor. The prolonged loneliness had actually made me approach people. Who knew? Back on Earth, I used to be more than happy to spend days on my own. But that was *days*, not months. There was just so long a person could be left on their own, even if they were an introvert like me.

Chapter 4

Kear

He walked Maya to her apartment after their lunch together, made sure she was safely inside, then finally went to his office.

For the rest of the day, he focused on his work, not giving much thought to their encounter.

Kear thrived on routine. It kept him focused, which facilitated accomplishment. All his daily activities strictly followed a predetermined plan. Taking almost an hour out of his schedule for lunch with Maya had shifted the rest of the items on his list, forcing him to catch up.

Despite that, he finished work only half an hour later than usual. The rest of his nightly activities still happened on time.

At six thirty, he left the office and took the elevator up to the top floor of the same hospital wing as his clinic. His personal suite took up two top floors of the wing, with several covered terraces adding to his living space. It was extremely convenient to work and live in the same building. Of course, that also meant he hardly ever left the hospital grounds, but he saw that as a benefit.

At seven, he ate dinner—alone, like always, while sitting at his desk.

At nine, he read for an hour—mostly the peer-reviewed articles from one of the several medical publications he subscribed to.

At ten, he closed the journal, used the bathroom, and changed into his pajamas.

By ten thirty, he was in bed.

Normally, he'd fall asleep to the vision of charts, numbers, and plans for the next day floating through his brain.

Tonight, however, his brain decided to focus on Maya. He hoped she was also in bed, getting the necessary rest. But what if she wasn't?

He never learned what had upset her. What kind of news had she received from home that had made her cry so inconsolably?

What if she was crying again right now?

What if she hadn't eaten her dinner?

Unable to relax, he got up, grabbed his tablet from the shelf by his bed and checked the hospital drone record. The dinner had been delivered to her apartment on time. But did she actually eat it?

Sleep deserted him completely. He sat on the bed, wondering what to do. He could call her apartment. But what if she *was* in bed and sleeping already? The call would wake her up and disrupt her natural cycle, which wouldn't be good for her or for his charts the next morning.

Of course, if she wasn't sleeping, it wasn't good either.

He got up and paced in a circle around his bed, running his hand through the fur on his head. The best thing would be to check on her in person. After all, she was in the same building, just a short elevator ride down.

Having made the decision, he left his suite. He'd make sure Maya was all right, then they both could get some sleep.

When he reached her place, he leaned with his ear against her door.

And jumped back.

The sharp noise of punches, followed by weapon blasts came from behind the door.

Was Maya being attacked?

His military training kicked in. He got into position, ready to break the door down.

Then, a commentary came from behind the door. Maya's television unit was on, he realized. She was watching a war documentary by the sound of it. Which meant she was still up. But she should be sound asleep at this hour.

Then, another sound came. A loud wail, interrupted by shuddering sobs. The woman was at it again. His worries turned out to be well-warranted. His subject was in distress and crying.

He had to put a stop to this.

Hitting the AI button by the door, he barked into the unit, "Professor Thormus here."

It took her some time to respond.

"Professor?" Her voice finally came through the communication unit by the door, though she didn't turn the video screen on. "Is everything all right?"

No. Obviously, it was not. Something was terribly wrong with his most important study subject. And he had to get to the bottom of it.

"Maya, can you open the door please?"

"Um..."

"It's important."

"Okay. Just give me a second."

Shoving a hand onto the doorframe, he hovered over it, waiting for what felt like an eternity. He was seriously considering kicking the fucking door down after all when it finally opened, though not very wide.

Maya poked her head out. She'd washed her face, but it remained obvious she'd been crying. The whites of her eyes looked red.

Did she always have such dark irises?

He paused, stunned for a moment. Voranian eyes came in many different colors, but he'd never seen any that looked like Maya's. Her irises were the darkest shade of brown, almost drowning her black pupils. And he suddenly felt like he was drowning, too, absorbed by their bottomless depth.

"Professor? Are you okay?" She glanced down his white, long pajamas.

He hadn't even thought about at least putting a robe on when rushing out to check on her. What was wrong with him? He'd never acted so irrationally before.

"Me?" He blinked. "Yes. I'm fine. But what about *you?* You should be in bed."

She gave him an incredulous look.

"Is that why you're here? To put me to bed?"

"Yes."

If she was so irresponsible as to neglect her daily schedule, he had to correct that. Even if it meant personally putting her to bed.

She kept staring at him in disbelief.

"You were crying again, Maya," he reprimanded.

Her thick, dark eyelashes dropped, shielding her reddened eyes.

"Something happened today, didn't it?" he prodded.

She lowered her head, avoiding looking at him.

"What is it, Maya?" he insisted. "What can I do to make it better?"

To his horror, a loud sob tore from her throat. She flung herself at him, wrapping her arms around his middle and burying her face in his chest. Whole-body shudders rocked her as she bawled loudly, no longer hiding her distress.

Utterly stunned, he stood rod-straight, his arms at his sides. He halted his breath, unsure what to do.

He'd faced death more times than he cared to count. He'd fought *fescods*, sometimes with not much more than his bare hands and horns. But there was nothing, absolutely nothing, that terrified him more than a crying woman.

This was the worst situation. And he had no idea how to handle it.

Slowly, ever so slowly, he forced his arms to move around her, finally enclosing her in a hug. He had never hugged a person in his life, other than his father and brothers. And even then, it had been just a firm, quick embrace, followed by a pat on the back or shoulder.

Never in his life had he had to hold someone for this long. He tried a small pat on her back, hoping she'd take it as a signal to let him go. But she only clung to him harder. The gentle swell of her belly pressed against his crotch with a rather unsettling sensation. Her body felt warm against his front, making him severely aware of the contact.

It was extremely awkward, but not entirely unpleasant.

She felt warm. Her hair smelled nice, similar to the berries in the drink he'd let her have at lunch today. It looked so thick and glossy. He'd never touched hair before. Voranians had fur. Ravils, the people of the planet Tragul where he'd fought during the war, had beautiful wavy hair, but he'd certainly never held any of them like this.

Lifting his hand, he ran it down the length of her hair, from her head down her back. A shudder shook her body as she pressed herself closer to him, crying uncontrollably. But somehow, he sensed it was working. His touch was welcome.

They stood like that in the doorway, his hooves across the threshold from her feet. He kept stroking her hair, falling into an odd rhythm with her sobbing. The longer he held her, the less awkward it felt. His body eased around hers. And little by little, her sobs lessened. She was running out of tears.

He'd never thought he was capable of consoling anyone. But he wasn't even *trying* to console her. He simply was there for her, letting her cry on his chest for as long as she needed. And somehow, it proved enough.

Miraculously, she stopped shaking and stilled, resting against him. The next moment, she sniffed and jerked away.

"I'm sorry." She sniffed again, rubbing her eyes. "I didn't mean to... I come from a big family of huggers. We 'hug out' all our problems..." She attempted a smile through her tears.

He disliked her apologizing for finding comfort in him. The awkwardness returned with a vengeance, and he didn't know what to say. All words felt wrong for the situation.

He pulled out a sanitary wipe from his pocket and shoved it into her hand.

"Here."

Chapter 5

Maya

I grabbed the soft, moist napkin the professor had offered and wiped my face. He immediately produced another one from his pocket. He must carry packs of these wipes everywhere with him, even to bed. Because judging by his pajamas that was exactly where he'd come from.

"Thanks." I took the napkin from him and blew my nose. I must look like a total mess.

A huge wet stain now graced the professor's pristine white pajamas over his chest. Embarrassment flooded me. I'd completely lost it and slobbered all over his clothes. I couldn't even look him in the eyes now.

"Come inside, Maya." Placing his hands on my shoulders, he walked me backward into the apartment.

After kicking my door shut with his hoof, he took the soiled napkins from me. Lifting them by their corners between his thumb and his finger, he placed them in the disposal unit by the door.

He looked calm and collected, like always—a stark contrast to the sobbing, quivering mess I'd been. Strolling to the television unit, he turned it off. The noise of the battle taking place on the screen ceased.

His gaze fell on the empty cupcake box on the couch. He flinched but didn't say anything. Lifting the box in a similar manner that he'd handled the dirty napkins with, he took it to the disposal unit and tossed it in.

"Let's get you ready for bed now," he said softly, then led me to the small bathroom off my living room. "Can I trust you to wash your face and brush your teeth on your own? Or should I do it for you?" There was no mocking or depreciation in his calm, detached voice of a doctor.

He really sounded like he'd brush my teeth for me if I said I couldn't do it.

I must look like a complete failure to him right now, incapable of taking care of myself.

"I'll do it." I headed for the sink with determination to pull myself together.

He nodded, stepping out of the bathroom and closing the door behind him.

I half expected him to be gone by the time I got out. But after I finished in the bathroom, I found the professor in my bedroom fluffing my pillows and turning down the cover.

I was so used to seeing Professor Thormus exclusively in the setting of the clinic's examination room. He'd storm in, looking all business. During the entire exam, he'd keep his focus on my uterus, on the screens of the devices, or on the notes on his tablet. Before today, he'd probably never even looked at me above my waist.

Pausing in the door to my bedroom, I admired the view of this large, strong man fluffing a pillow for my comfort. I tried to remember when I'd last had anyone in my apartment. It was probably when the representative of the Liaison Committee, Alcus Hecear, came to check on me last month. He didn't come into my bedroom, of course. We just sat on the couch, had some tea, and talked.

The professor noticed me standing in the doorway.

"Where are your pajamas, Maya?"

"I don't have any."

His thick eyebrows jerked up in shock.

"You don't?"

"The contract stated not to bring any clothes with me," I explained. "I can only wear what is provided to me by the clinic."

It provided an unlimited supply of white hospital gowns and robes, but nothing else. After brushing my teeth in the bathroom, I'd changed into a fresh gown and robe, getting rid of those stained with cupcake icing and the dirt from crawling in the flower bed earlier today.

The professor rubbed the back of his neck. "The contract does stipulate that, doesn't it?"

I nodded. "I sleep in a hospital gown."

I took the robe off, careful not to turn my back to him. The gown was open on the back from the waist down. It was very convenient for the daily exams of my nether regions. But outside of the lab, I had no desire to flash my naked butt at the professor.

He shifted on his hooves uneasily, then cleared his throat and patted the mattress.

"All right, then. Off to bed with you."

I climbed under the covers.

"Thank you, Professor," I said sleepily as he tucked the blankets around me. The exhaustion of the day had caught up with me, and the sugar rush from the cupcakes was wearing off. "You're a warm, kind person. We should hang out more."

Now, I wished I'd had the guts to speak with him earlier. Who knew Professor Thormus would actually turn out to be such a nice guy? He'd always seemed so cold and unapproachable. But there he was, tucking me into bed, like a loving older brother, after comforting me through a massive meltdown. Clearly, appearances could be deceiving.

He grunted and patted my shoulder through the covers.

"Just get some rest, Maya. I'll lock the door on my way out."

Chapter 6

Kear

"*You're a warm, kind person.*"

That was something he'd never heard anyone say to him before.

Kind?

Well, he wasn't evil. He never hurt anyone on purpose, other than the *fescods*. But he wasn't selflessly kind in the conventional sense of the word. He wouldn't go out of his way to help a stranger, mostly because he rarely noticed them. He'd grown to view people as either troublesome or bothersome, and he'd learned to generally ignore them, staying away from them whenever possible.

Warm?

That was an even worse word to describe him.

He'd been avoiding any "warm" feelings all his life. In his line of work, it was often necessary. He couldn't allow himself to *feel* when he was doing his work because then sorrow for every life he'd lost would destroy him.

He lingered by Maya's door. Pressing his ear to it, he listened for any sound behind it, like more sobbing or the noise of her getting up again to eat another box of those *cupcakes*.

How much sugar was in them? The fur on the back of his neck rose when he thought about the havoc it must have wreaked on her system.

How did she even get her hands on those? He didn't allow them in his clinic. A part of him urged him to launch an investigation and put an end to her supply source.

Another, more rational part, realized he couldn't possibly control her every single action. Stuffing her face with *cupcakes* clearly was a coping mechanism. Something upset her so much, she disregarded the nutritional requirements outlined in the contract she'd signed. His cutting her off from sugar would not make her feel any better. He had to look at the root of the problem to fix it. And the *root* had something to do with the news she got from back home. He needed to find out what it was.

Satisfied that Maya safely stayed in bed and, hopefully, would be soundly asleep soon, he stomped back to his place and made his house AI call Alcus Hecear.

He remembered how late it was only when the screen of his house drone showed the sleepy face of the representative against a pillow in the dark room.

"Professor Kear Umhra Thormus?" Even half-asleep, Alcus wouldn't forget his manners or drop the formalities, using Kear's full name and title as per the custom in Voran. "Is something wrong with Madam Maya Gupta?"

"No. Um, yes." Kear paced his spacious living room, the house drone following him closely.

Alcus slipped out of his bed and sneaked out of his bedroom, quietly closing the door behind him. He obviously realized this would be a lengthy conversation and didn't want to wake his boyfriend, who must be asleep.

"Do you need me to come to the hospital?" Alcus asked, rubbing his eyes, his sleeping mask dangling from one of his horns.

The fur on the representative's head was a mess, and his horns were bare of paint. That fact struck Kear the most. He'd never seen Alcus with undecorated horns before.

"Is it urgent, Professor?"

"Yes. Very urgent."

"What's happening? Where is she?" Alcus ripped his pajama top off, heading to his dressing room.

"In her apartment. In her bed."

"Alone? What is she doing?"

"Sleeping."

"Sleeping?" Alcus paused in his struggle with putting a shirt on over his head while the sleeping mask got tangled in it. "Maya is sleeping?"

"Yes." Kear ran a hand over his forehead, suddenly realizing how ridiculous he sounded, dragging poor Alcus out of bed over a box of eaten *cupcakes*.

"Professor?" Alcus sat on a chair in his dressing room. Dropping his shirt into his lap, he blinked in confusion. "If Maya is safely asleep in her bed, why do you need me at the hospital?"

Good question.

Kear heaved a breath.

Maya was his work. His career depended on the outcome of this study. It was important, very much so. But he had never lost his mind over his work before. Everything concerning her unsettled him so much, he really acted like he'd lost his mind.

"All right," he said. "No need to rush, I guess. Could you talk to her tomorrow, though? She was very upset today. I found her crying."

He should've called Alcus right after lunch, instead of believing Maya's reassurances that she'd be fine. Alcus was so much better equipped to deal with upset females than Kear ever hoped to be.

"She was crying?" Alcus looked alarmed again. "Why? What happened?"

"I found her in the rooftop gardens with her tablet. She got some upsetting news from home. Alcus, I need to know what the news was."

"Why didn't you ask her?"

Because he feared the questions would make her break down again.

"I will," he said. "Eventually. But I need to know what's happening right now, so I can design a plan to handle it. I need access to Maya's communications."

Alcus pursed his mouth.

"That would be a violation of her privacy."

"No," Kear argued. "The communication affected the physical and emotional wellbeing of my study subject. As such, it falls under the factors influencing my research as covered in the contract. I need to know all the factors."

Alcus shook his head. The sleeping mask dangled like a swing off his horn, hitting him in the face. He winced and finally yanked it off.

"What does it matter, Professor? You won't be able to do anything about whatever happened back on Earth."

"But I will be able to mitigate the damage the bad news has on her. From now on, I want all Maya's communication directed to me."

"And what would that accomplish? You can't possibly sever her connection with her home world. Your contract already disallows the use of social media. Electronic letters are her only link with her family."

"I'm not saying I'll cut that link off, Alcus. I just need to know in advance what we're dealing with to have time to adequately prepare her for the bad news and, hopefully, mitigate the impact they have on her."

Alcus scratched behind his ear, pondering his request.

"She would need to know about it. You have to tell her you'll be intercepting all her messages. I suspect she'll object to that."

"She may. But communication with Earth generally isn't a private matter, Representative. All earthlings in Voran know it." For security reasons, all messages from Earth went through the Liaison Committee. AI scanned them first, but the representatives also read them if AI flagged them. "Maya knew when she signed the contract that it came with far more restrictions than the standard marriage agreement between our planets. This study is bigger than you or me, Alcus. It's bigger than her, too."

"I'm not minimizing the importance of your work, Professor, or the impact it has on our society. But my job is to ensure Maya is happy on Neron."

"Then, our goals are the same, Representative. I, too, wish for nothing more than Maya's happiness." Or, as it was worded in the contract, *the subject's emotional and physical wellbeing.* "On that note, I need to see the last message she received from home."

"Now?"

"Yes." He wouldn't be able to fall asleep, anyway. If he tried to focus on work, he'd think back to this again and again, because Maya *was* his work.

"But—"

"Listen, Maya already read that message. The damage is done. Now, I need to know what she's dealing with, because now I'm dealing with the consequences of it, too."

"Well..." Alcus finally relented, either faced with Kear's impeccable logic or simply worn out by his stubbornness. "If it's for her own good."

"It most certainly is."

Chapter 7

Kear

What a poor fucking excuse of a man!

Maya had the misfortune to have absolute scum for a boyfriend. The coward couldn't wait for a few more months to break up with her face-to-face. He had to do it to her over interstellar communication, while she was pregnant, away from home and her usual support system.

Kear knew next to nothing about intimate relationships. He prided himself on successfully avoiding them all his life. It saved him so much angst and inevitable heartache, allowing him to focus all his energy on his work.

His sex life consisted solely of regular visits to a massage spa to use the pods for relief once a week. The machines took care of his physical needs, leaving his emotions intact. But even he realized how heartless a move that was on Maya's boyfriend's part.

Now, Kear and his team had a real situation on their hands.

Alcus Hecear was going to be here in the morning. The man had lots of experience in handling the matters of the heart. He'd help Maya straighten out her emotions. That'd be a good start.

But Kear would have to take it from there. He had to find a way to keep Maya happy. No more *cupcakes*. But maybe he could let her have another ice milk?

She'd mentioned something about "hanging out more often." Maybe he could take her somewhere outside of the hospital building? As an exception to the rules.

Summer was here. All outdoor parks were now open. Or he could take her shopping and buy her some pajamas, since it was his fault she didn't have any. First, of course, he'd have to buy her something to wear other than the hospital robe so she could leave here in the first place.

He rubbed his forehead. He'd thought that he'd been keeping his subject safe, that he had accounted for all harmful factors. Now, he had to rethink and adjust his strategy. It took some thought, time, and effort, but it could be done.

At least now, he could get back to bed and sleep for a few hours before his alarm went off.

He was about to turn off the screen with the letter from the asshole boyfriend when his tablet dinged with a new message. It was another letter arriving from the human guy's account.

Irritation flared in Kear's chest. What did he want from Maya? Hadn't he done enough? Couldn't he leave her alone now?

Maybe the idiot had thought it through and reconsidered?

That'd be good. After all, who in their own mind would want to break up with Maya? She was so...um... Granted, Kear didn't know much about her as a person. But she didn't deserve what her boyfriend did to her. It took a special kind of asshole to make a woman cry like that.

If the boyfriend wanted to reconcile, however, that would make Maya happy. And if she was happy, Kear was ready to forgive her boyfriend, too.

He hit the read-aloud button so his translator would be able to convey the meaning of the letter to him.

"Hi Pooh Bear. I hope you're faring well. It's never easy to break up a ten-year-long relationship. It surely took a toll on me. I can't stop thinking about it. I know it's for the best, but I'm not sure I did it in the best way possible."

Ha, you think?

"Rhea believes I should've explained better where I was coming from. You see, we're in love, and we want to give our relationship the best chance without anything dragging us down."

Wait... What?

Any idea of sleep blown away, Kear paced his living room once again as the drone kept reading out loud.

"Apparently, Rhea has loved me since the moment she met me. Remember the picnic where you introduced us, back in high school?"

So, that Rhea person was Maya's friend from school?

It just went from bad to worse.

"About seven months ago, Rhea got a new job and moved to our neighborhood. We've been together ever since. You see, Pooh Bear, it was destiny."

Destiny?

And Maya apparently stood in the way of it—"dragging it down"—that was why the asshole dumped her.

Good riddance, as far as Kear was concerned, but all these new revelations would surely devastate Maya.

And what kind of stupid nickname was that? *Pooh Bear?* Why would anyone refer to their loved one as "excrement of a large predator?" Or was it a "defecating predator?" Either way, it was disgusting. Unless the translator messed it up. Or maybe the boyfriend meant it as an insult? In which case, Kear's blood boiled with anger and indignation for Maya.

He hadn't been so enraged since... Well, never. Even when he had fought *fescods* during the war, he viewed them as a threat to be eliminated. He wasn't enraged at every *fescod* he'd killed.

Now, he was seething with anger at a man he'd never even met.

Oh, how he *wished* to meet that guy so he could personally punch his hornless face and kick his tail-less ass.

How did that idiot even think that it was a good idea to keep writing to Maya after what he'd done to her yesterday? Now, he was just poking the wound he'd inflicted, with all the confessions that she hadn't asked him for.

"I just want you to know I completely understand where you're coming from, asking me to wait until you come back. But waiting wouldn't be fair to you. It'd just prolong the inevitable. I feel that letting you know the truth is the right thing to do. I just want to be honest..."

Honest? After seeing this other woman behind Maya's back for seven months, *now* he suddenly wished to be honest?

That was more than Kear could take.

"Reply," he barked at the drone, his tail lashing wildly. "Listen here, you asshole!" he dictated. "You're a disgusting, lying piece of shit. How dare you do this to Maya when you're perfectly aware of her condition?"

Oh, it felt so good to let everything he thought about that asshole off his chest. Almost as good as punching him would've been. He kept dictating and by the time he finished, he felt winded, like after one of his morning sessions with the exercise robot.

"Send?" the drone inquired.

Sending this would feel even more satisfying. But if he sent his long, angry letter to Maya's boyfriend, she'd learn about it too, which would probably upset her even more. It'd stir the drama and potentially prolong her heartache. Not to mention that he risked an interplanetary conflict if the boyfriend complained to the authorities. Which the whiny piece of shit probably would do after getting everything Kear thought about him put ever so eloquently in writing.

He heaved a breath and exhaled it slowly.

"No. Delete it. The whole thing."

"Deleted," the AI drone confirmed.

Kear had to do *something*, though. He couldn't let the new message hurt Maya all over again in the morning. She'd probably check for it the moment she woke up, and it'd hurt her.

Fuck. It would hurt her badly.

Even as an emotionally secure person as Kear had made himself, he realized the potential damage it'd do to Maya to learn that her boyfriend of ten years had been cheating on her with her friend from school. The way that asshole wrote about "destiny" and them being in love would make the blow even more devastating.

The letter also mentioned something about Maya "asking" her boyfriend to wait with the breakup. She must've replied to his previous message.

At this point, however, any further communication with her ex-boyfriend was nothing but harmful. Kear had to stop it.

Using his access to the Liaison Committee system and the expanded clearance granted to him by Alcus Hecear tonight, he recalled the boyfriend's last message and blocked it from reaching Maya. After that, he blocked his entire account to prevent any future messages to her, too. There was no need for him to contact her ever again. The asshole could wax poetic about destiny elsewhere.

Feeling a little calmer, Kear finally stomped into his bedroom and climbed into bed. He might be able to salvage about an hour or two of sleep still.

As he lay in bed, however, thoughts of Maya wouldn't leave him.

She'd written to her useless boyfriend. She'd expect a response, and when it didn't come, she'd be worried. Letting her see his last message would be a mistake. However, leaving her without a reply wasn't the best option, either.

This was a lose-lose situation.

Tossing the covers aside, he sat up in bed once again, racking his sleep-deprived brain for what to do. What would be the best outcome for Maya here?

The best would be a message from her boyfriend writing to her that his first email was a mistake. That he actually loved her. A lot.

But that wasn't going to happen. At best, her good-for-nothing boyfriend should've kept his stupid "honesty" to himself for just a few months longer. He should've waited until Maya was no longer pregnant and exceptionally vulnerable. Until she was back home, among humans again, surrounded by her family and friends. Then, he could've had this unpleasant conversation with her face-to-face.

Kear knew nothing about romance. He didn't know Maya that well, either. But he believed she deserved that much after putting up with that asshole for ten years.

Instead, the coward chose to break up with her long-distance. And now, he kept poking the poor woman where it hurt, writing to her about his cheating.

Since there was no hope the man was willing or even capable of rectifying the situation, Kear had to do it for him.

"New message," he announced to the drone. "Dear Maya..."

He decided against using the Pooh Bear moniker, just in case it *was* an insult.

"Upon further consideration, I have come to the decision to rescind my previous communication..."

That sounded like one of the letters to a medical publication he'd written over the years, not something a man would write to a woman.

The problem was, Kear had never written to a woman before. The best Kear could do was pretend he was writing to his father or to one of his brothers. Normally, they communicated by video when needed and got together for family celebrations. But he could pretend he had to write to someone from his family this once.

"Sorry, I made a mistake and sent that message too quickly. You're right. It's best to wait until you're back home. We'll talk then."

He made the drone read it to him out loud. It sounded simple and to the point.

"Perfect," he said.

"Send?" the AI inquired.

"Wait." He remembered the previous message to Maya was signed. "Put the name Walter as the signature and convert it to the Earth language."

"Which one? There are currently six thousand and five—"

"Whatever language was the last message you read to me in? Use that one."

"The language and the signature are confirmed. Send?"

"Wait." He stopped the AI again.

Using his tablet, he accessed the Liaison Committee's system once again. Here, he found Walter's account and configured it to connect with his. This way, when his message reached Maya, it would look like it came from fucking Walter, which is how it had to be.

It was for Maya's peace for now, he decided. She can deal with all this mess later, when she was in a much more stable situation back home and would be far better equipped to deal with it.

"Send," he ordered the AI.

When he went to bed again after that, he finally fell asleep and slept soundly for the whole twenty-three minutes until his alarm went off.

Chapter 8

Maya

"*Dear Maya... Sorry, I made a mistake.*"

I'd dreamed of seeing these words from Walter, but getting his letter that morning didn't make me feel much better. The letter was too short and sounded too formulaic, though I had no time to ponder what that could mean.

Alcus Hecear knocked on my door shortly after, about one hour before my morning exam. Dressed in the Liaison Committee's gold-and-white uniform, his long horns painted with yellow polka dots, a bright smile on his face, he was the picture of cheerful friendliness.

"Tea?" he asked, lifting the tray with tea and breakfast patties that were on the list of approved foods for me.

I blinked at him in confusion. "Isn't our meeting supposed to be next week?"

"It is. But I was in the area and decided to drop by for a chat, if it's alright with you?"

"Of course, it is."

I liked Alcus and wouldn't mind his company even if I wasn't generally starving for interaction as a result of this study that kept me in isolation. After a few minutes of chatting over tea, however, I realized it wasn't just a friendly visit. Alcus was too focused with his questions.

"Do you feel sad? Lonely?"

"Any signs of homesickness?"

"Do you wish for closer communication from back home?"

It sounded like a therapy session.

"Is it about the meltdown I had yesterday?" I finally asked.

He shifted on the cute, round couch in my small living area.

"Professor Thormus is worried," he said carefully. "He called me last night..."

Oh boy. As much as I'd tried not to make a big deal out of my personal life, it somehow had gotten out of control. Now, more people were involved.

"The professor has nothing to worry about. It was mostly hormones and stuff." I stroked my belly. It wasn't huge yet. I'd been told it might never get very big at all since it was my first pregnancy and the fetus was on the smaller side.

After the initial morning sickness and the weird gray patches on my legs that had turned out to be a harmless, temporary side effect of some Voranian substances introduced to my system, I hardly even felt pregnant.

I had to reassure Alcus a few more times that I was fine before he finally seemed to believe me.

"You know you can call me anytime, Madam Maya Gupta," he told me as we both headed for the door from my apartment.

It was almost the time for my exam, and I figured I might as well walk to the elevators with Alcus.

"Yes, thank you. I like talking to you," I smiled, opening the door and coming face to face with Professor Thormus himself. "Oh..."

"Good morning, Maya." He inclined his head. "Representative Alcus Hecear. Nice to see you here."

He didn't look surprised at finding Alcus in my place. They probably talked about him coming over when they spoke about me last night. It was to be expected since the Committee handled everything that involved humans in Voran, and Professor Thormus currently was in charge of everything that involved me.

There was not a trace left of the professor's hurried appearance from last night. This morning, he was his usual neat self—crisp white coverall and perfectly styled fur. Only his eyes searched mine with the same concern as before, and his arrow-tipped tail twitched a little, tapping the side of his leg.

"Did you want to make sure I made it out of bed okay?" I asked, still smiling.

He rubbed the back of his neck. "Just wanted to wish you a good morning. And bring you this." He shoved a bag into my hands.

"What is it?" I opened the bag, glimpsing some soft white material inside. "Is it a new hospital gown?" God knew, I had enough of those already.

"No." He cleared his throat, looking more uncomfortable than normal. "Though I did use the size of your hospital gown to order it. I hope it'll fit."

I pulled out a garment. "Are those pants?"

They were loose and long.

"And a shirt," he added.

"Pajamas? For me?" These looked like a pair of baggy pajamas. Still, a step up from a hospital gown. "Thanks."

I smiled wider. At least, these would keep my butt warm when I slept.

The professor shook his head. "No. These are clothes to wear when you go outside."

"Outside?" I couldn't believe my ears. "Am I allowed to leave here? Really?"

"For a little while," he conceded, somewhat reluctantly. "You wanted to see some of the City of Voran, so—"

"When?" I interrupted him. Excitement bubbled inside me already, making it hard to stand still.

"Whenever you wish."

"Today?"

"Um..." He shifted his weight to another hoof. "Well, today we have your medical exam—"

"But after? This afternoon, maybe? Or for lunch?"

Alcus moved his eyes from me to the professor.

"What an excellent idea, Professor Thormus," he gushed, catching my excitement. "It's going to be gorgeous weather today. A perfect day for an outing."

Chapter 9

Kear

"So, where are you taking me today?" Maya all but skipped at his side as he walked to his place after picking her up after lunch.

The loose-fitting pantsuit he'd chosen for her appeared to drown her figure in white fabric, but she didn't seem to mind. Her eyes shone with anticipation. She appeared to burst with excitement, finally getting the chance to go out.

Had he kept her locked in this hospital for way too long? It had been for her safety. The City of Voran wasn't particularly dangerous, but in Maya's unique situation, even the slightest incident could have devastating consequences. He simply couldn't take the risk.

It appeared, however, that the isolation he'd imposed on Maya had some negative effects, too. He had to tread delicately and find the optimal balance between safety and boredom.

"Can we go to a park?" she asked as they entered the elevator.

"I was thinking a shopping mall would be better for now, since you haven't been provided with a set of pajamas yet."

Come to think of it, the pantsuit he got for her looked very much like pajamas. He'd wanted her clothes to be soft and comfortable, but now, she looked like she was ready for bed, not a trip into the city.

"Shopping?" She clapped her hands. "How fun!"

He sensed she'd find anything fun at this point. He could've told her he was taking her to a waste processing facility, and she'd be just as excited. He winced at a pinch of guilt in his chest. Yes, he'd certainly overdone it with her isolation.

"How are we going to get there?" She matched her speed to his as they exited the elevator and headed down the corridor, nearly running at his side.

He slowed his steps, realizing her legs were much shorter than his.

"We'll fly. Like most people in this city do."

He stopped at his door and touched the AI screen mounted by the doorframe.

"Oooh." Maya's eyes grew wider as she entered his main room and slowly turned around. "What is this place?"

"It's my suite," he said, closing the front door behind them.

"You live here?" She walked between the glass pillars that were draped in flower garlands. "There are more flowers in here than anywhere else in the hospital."

"Rules on the amount and the kind of plants are different for private residences. My suite is not categorized as a medical facility. There are fewer restrictions."

The lower level of his place was open to the floor above that had a glass dome for a ceiling. Bright daylight flooded the space to the benefit of the flower garlands hanging from the two-story-high pillars and the indoor balconies above. Glass-covered terraces opened up the space from both ends to the right and the left of them. The kitchen, his workroom with some lab equipment, the sitting room, and another large room he had no purpose for occupied the lower level between the terraces.

Upstairs held his exercise room and several bedrooms, only one of which was furnished.

"This is gorgeous," Maya gushed. "Look at all these plants! It's like indoor gardens. Do you live here alone?"

"Yes."

"How do you not get lost? It's so much space!"

He mostly used only four rooms of the suite—his workroom, the exercise room, a bedroom, and a bathroom. It was easy *not* to get lost.

The sitting room was meant to be used for when he had visitors, which hardly ever happened.

His AI drone whirred their way. "Greetings, Professor. Greetings, visitor."

Maya perked up at the sight of the silver disk with shiny arms fitted with pincers.

"Hi." She gave the machine a small wave, then leaned toward Kear, lowering her voice. "What's his name?"

"*Whose* name?"

"Your house AI's? They usually have names. I saw it in Voranian movies."

"Right." He rubbed his left horn, wondering how he even ended up having this conversation. "Well, I didn't name mine. It has a factory ID number if I ever need to identify it."

"You call him by his ID number?" Eyes open wide, she gaped at him as if he'd just admitted to kicking cute little *ulto* pups for fun.

"*It* not *him,*" he corrected. The drone was a machine, after all. It had no gender. "And I don't call it anything. Why would I talk to a machine, other than to give it orders?"

"Well…" She shrugged. "You live alone and have no one else to talk to. Why not?"

"Do *you* talk to the hospital AI?" Every patient room had a drone centrally operated by the hospital AI.

"Of course I do. I'm not allowed to program his name in the system, since he isn't mine, but I gave him a name anyway."

"You gave the hospital AI a name?" Well, the woman really was out of this world.

She nodded. "I call my drone Mani."

"Why Mani?"

"It was the name of the dog we had when I was little. My dad says it means 'jewel.'"

"Jewel?" He eyed his house drone that looked more like a loose part of a spaceship than any jewel. Clearly, the woman had an overactive imagination. "Alright then."

"So, what's upstairs?" She gestured at the balcony of the second floor above.

"A few bedrooms with bathrooms."

"A few?" Her dark eyebrows rose. "How many do you need?"

"Just one. But the rest came with the place." It wasn't like he could annex all the unnecessary rooms from the suite.

Staying focused with her proved challenging. Her questions kicked his mind off all established tracks. He also found himself distracted by watching the ever-changing expressions on her face that hid nothing.

She was distracting, but also oddly stimulating in the ways he hadn't experienced before. He wouldn't mind staying here and listening to her nonsense about giving names to inanimate objects. But he'd already changed his afternoon schedule to accommodate this shopping trip. He should at least adhere to the altered schedule now.

"We need to go, Maya. Come, the landing pad is this way."

Her brows slid up even higher, but she nodded. "Of course, you have your own landing pad."

"Many people do. Where else would they park their aircraft?"

He took her out to the open terrace.

With most buildings in Voran City being tower-tall, flying was the most common way of traveling. Most people owned a personal aircraft to get around. Granted, not everyone had an aircraft as slick and as fast as his.

For someone who only left the hospital building when he couldn't avoid it, there was no need to have an aircraft like that. Buying it was an indulgence on his part. He reasoned that if he had to leave his house, he might as well use something fast enough to get him there and back promptly. That it was easy on the eyes didn't hurt either.

"Nice." Maya slid a hand over the smooth, red front panel inside, then slightly bounced in the cushioned seat.

"Are you comfortable?" he asked, bringing the aircraft into motion.

"As comfy as could be." She grinned, twisting her head around to look out through the transparent body of the aircraft.

He hit the destination button, and the craft took the course toward the largest shopping mall in the city.

"Wow." Maya pressed her nose to the glass, taking in the sights slowly drifting by below. "This looks even better than in a movie."

"You've seen this before, on your flight from the space port after your arrival."

"Yes. But I felt rather overwhelmed that day to pay attention to details. There was so much to absorb upon arrival on an alien planet. Besides, it was already covered in snow when I got here. Everything's so green now."

Topped with glass domes, the high buildings of Voran City rose into the blue sky. Most of the glass bubbles of covered terraces and balconies were open due to the balmy weather. Greenery, so beloved by his people, was everywhere. Vines with flowers draped over lattices and railings. Shrubs and trees grew from the pots. Rooftop gardens burst with spring flowers, and the outdoor park had already sprouted enough green to cover the dirt and eliminate every remnant of winter.

"It's a nice day," he had to agree.

After a few minutes of being glued to the glass of the aircraft, Maya finally settled into her seat, looking straight ahead.

He glanced at the control panel in front of him. "We should be there in about fifteen minutes."

She dipped her gaze to his hands resting in his lap. "You're not flying it? The guys in movies usually do."

He chuckled. "The guys in movies like to show off. I can hand-fly it if I had to, too, but I don't need to do it to prove my worth as a man.

Besides, it's safer to let the AI fly it," he assured her, wondering if fear might be the reason for her suddenly subdued mood.

Her eyes still darted around, taking in the new sights, but the happy bubbliness of earlier had dimmed.

Instead of enjoying the unexpected quiet, it bothered him.

"How have you been lately?" he asked, trying to keep his voice casual. Sadly, casual conversations weren't on the extensive list of his skills.

She glanced at him suspiciously.

"You tell me, Professor. You're the one with probes and charts. Is everything going as expected?"

"I'm not talking about the pregnancy, Maya. I'm asking about *you*. How are you doing?"

"What does it matter?" She shrugged a shoulder.

"It matters very much. You are the subject of my study. The most important part of it."

"Ah," she snapped. "So, it is about the pregnancy, after all."

He blew out a breath. Somehow it seemed easier talking to her before.

Searching for words carefully, he tried again. "I just wonder how you feel and if—"

She closed her eyes, running a hand over her face.

"I'm sorry, Professor. I didn't mean to be rude. It's just that Alcus turned his morning visit into some kind of therapy session with the same 'How are you?' questions. And now you..."

"I only inquired—" He used to be proud of his eloquent writing and public-speaking skills. Yet there he was tripping over his words with her.

It wasn't pleasant to learn he wasn't that good with words after all, at least not enough to casually talk to a woman. An attractive woman, he had to add. Maybe that was the problem? He hadn't felt attracted to a patient before.

He heaved a heavy breath, afraid to think about all the implications of that discovery. Maya just happened to be pleasant to look at. That didn't mean he found her attractive.

Or did it?

She bit her lip, fidgeting with the hem of her shirt. "It's not your fault. It's just that I don't know what to say or how to answer those questions."

"Say it as is. I'll listen."

She drew in a long breath, then released it slowly before giving him a penetrating look. He waited, hoping she'd open up.

"I received a...a rather unpleasant message from home," she blurted out in a halting string of words.

"Just one?"

That meant her boyfriend's second letter hadn't reached her. He had managed to stop it in time.

It'd been a wrong question to ask, he realized, as she glanced at him with confusion.

"I mean...you've been upset for a while now." He shut his mouth, afraid to make things worse if he kept talking.

"I know," she said hesitantly. "I probably should explain my melt-down."

"Probably." That was all he trusted himself to say this time.

"My...boyfriend," she swallowed, taking a brief pause to compose herself. Before continuing. "He, um... decided he'd rather be single than have a long-distance relationship with me."

Not *single*. The asshole had already found another girlfriend, close to home. But Kear would die before he told Maya that.

"I'm sorry," he said, measuring his words like a miser would money. The less he said, the better.

"Thanks." She heaved a sigh, but at least she wasn't crying. Yet. "Long distance is hard on relationships. I knew that. But I hoped..." Her voice broke, her eyes turning glossy.

Shit, she was about to cry again.

"Maya…" He reached for her instinctively, without having a fucking clue how to handle this.

"I'm fine." She patted his hand reassuringly. "I'm much better today. Promise." She smiled, but her eyes remained shiny with unshed tears. "Apparently, he's having second thoughts."

"He is?" She got his message! "It's good then, isn't it?"

"Honestly? I don't even know what to think."

Oh no, this wasn't the reaction he'd hoped for when sending that letter to her yesterday.

"Why?"

She chewed on her bottom lip. "It was a very weird message."

"Why?" he repeated like a dummy.

"Short, impersonal. He addressed me by my name."

"And that's wrong? How?"

"Walter only ever uses my name when he's angry or irritated with me."

Well, that was a problem. He'd made a mistake by not talking to her first to learn all these things.

"What did he call you when he wasn't angry?"

She cast her eyes down, a tiny smile playing on her lips. "He had a bunch of silly nicknames for me."

"Like what?"

"Oh, the usual. Babe, sweetie, and such…" She waved a hand in a vague gesture, her voice trailing off.

"Do you like the nicknames?" How could any reasonable person appreciate being called *Pooh Bear?*

"Some more than others." She shrugged. "But it's mostly the tone of voice that matters, not the nickname, isn't it?"

"Not if the message is written," he thought.

"The point is that he didn't use any nicknames this time," she continued. "The whole letter was just like two lines when he used to write me pages before. Now I wonder why he even bothered. Clearly, he isn't into me anymore."

Her chin trembled, and she glanced away quickly, fighting the tears. Relieved, he saw she won that fight just a moment later, looking at him again relatively calmly.

He had to figure out how it worked between people in a relationship. "So, a longer letter from this ass... I mean, your *boyfriend* would be better? Would it make you happier if he wrote more?"

"Well, it also depends on the content of the letter, of course. But yes, if he changed his mind and decided to wait until I'm back on Earth, then I would like to see him put all his reasoning behind his decision into that letter. After all, he took the time to write a very long one, telling why he was breaking up with me in the first place. He owes me an explanation on why he has changed his mind all of a sudden."

That was another mistake Kear made. The letters from the human male were long and detailed. The guy probably talked a lot, too, loving to hear himself speak. Kear should've taken that into consideration when posing as him.

"So, a longer letter, with an explanation, using nicknames, would make you happy?" he summed it up out loud.

"Yes. Like a man in love would write, you know? Not like a lawyer contacting his client about something."

And not like a scientist, pretending to write to his father. Apparently, he sucked in casual correspondence just as much as in casual conversation.

"Sorry, I unloaded it all on you." She petted his hand again. "It's not something you should concern yourself with."

Oh, he was concerned. Very much so.

"I'll write him back," she said suddenly. "We'll see what he says."

Well, shit.

"You will?"

But why did he think she wouldn't?

How did he assume that telling her to wait with the break-up would make her cease all correspondence with her boyfriend?

Last night, Kear's sleep-deprived brain failed to consider the simple possibility that a woman would want to keep in touch with the man she thought she loved even if they agreed to "wait and see" with their relationship.

"Is that it?" Maya rose in her seat, pointing at the cluster of giant glass domes of the Central Mall.

"That's it," he confirmed as the aircraft descended toward the parking platform.

Chapter 10

Maya

The sights, the smells, the sounds!

It was so exciting to be out.

The shopping center looked like a gigantic indoor market. Storefronts lined the wide aisles on either side under a high glass ceiling decorated with arches of flowers. Where the aisles crossed, plazas formed. They looked like small town squares, complete with water features and dining areas under gazebos.

"I love it here." I grinned at the professor.

He didn't smile back. Firmly holding my elbow, he maneuvered us between the groups of Voranians strolling by. Every now and then, people would stop to stare at us, but he ignored everyone. His lips pressed tightly, his eyes narrowed, he looked like a man on a mission, avoiding eye contact with anyone.

"Where should we go first?" I asked.

"Pajamas," he bit out one word.

"A clothing store then?"

"Right."

As much as I disliked crowds, I didn't mind mingling with people after the long, boring months in the hospital. The poor professor, however, seemed extremely uncomfortable in his skin right now.

"Professor Kear Umhra Thormus!" a Voranian man shouted, rushing down the wide hall toward us.

The professor grunted softly, his fingers on my arm flexing.

The man grabbed his free hand into both of his. "I'm a huge fan of your work."

"Thanks, but I'm not a movie star. I don't have fans."

"Oh yes, you do." The man chuckled, shaking his head, as if he'd heard a joke. He then turned to me. "Madam Maya Gupta. It's so nice to meet you in person. You are my hero."

"I am?" I blinked, lost for words.

"My sister is on her third pregnancy. Another set of triplets!" he announced proudly. "She is so nervous. Her second pregnancy had some complications, she barely made it out alive. But she decided to go ahead with the third one, for a dear friend of hers. He's been dying to become a father—"

The professor's expression darkened. "What kind of complications?"

"Um..." The man rubbed his right horn awkwardly. "I'm not sure about the exact medical terms—"

"I'd like to see your sister as soon as possible," the professor fired off. "In my clinic. Tell her to say I sent her when she comes to reception."

The man looked stunned.

"Oh... Wow. Thanks... I really don't know what to say..."

"Goodbye." The professor steered me into the entrance of the closest store.

"That was nice of you," I said softly as he led me between the racks of clothes and away from the man.

His expression didn't ease, even as we got completely out of sight from anyone in the main hall of the mall. His shoulders squared, his grip remained firm on my arm.

"Professor? Are you alright?" Hearing about past pregnancy complications of a woman he'd never met couldn't have upset him so. "Do you know that man? Or his sister?"

"No." He stopped in his tracks.

Letting go of my arm, he ran his hands through the fur on his head.

"But she shouldn't have pushed her luck with the third one."

"You think three are too many?"

"The number isn't the problem. Some women can do just fine with more than that. But some..." He rubbed his chest through the white shirt he wore. "My mother didn't survive even one."

"Oh no..." I stared at him. "I'm so sorry, Professor. I...I didn't know."

That might be another reason he'd chosen this career path—his mother died while giving birth to him. He wanted to make sure it never happened to anyone else.

Professor Thormus cared about his patients far more than he let people know, more than he possibly wanted to care.

He nodded, acknowledging my sympathy and squared his shoulders.

"It was a long time ago. There have been great advancements in medicine since."

My mind was still reeling from his revelation. "Your father must've been devastated. And you... You grew up without a mother."

"Like most children in Voran do," he pointed out. "Maya, you feel too much for others. But there is no need to feel sorry for me or for my father. Yes, he was devastated by her death, but my mother had broken his heart many times over before that. Though it wasn't really her fault."

"Were they married?"

"No. He proposed to her many times, but she turned him down again and again, until she married someone else."

"Oh, that's..." I felt lost for words, but the professor finished for me.

"*That* is a typical situation in Voran where women often have many options, forcing men to compete for their attention. I deliberately chose to avoid putting myself into that situation."

The wall of clothes suddenly parted.

"Can I help you find what you're looking for?" A cheerful woman greeted us, shoving the clothes aside.

The professor cleared his throat, promptly schooling his expression back to neutral.

"Yes. We need a pair of pajamas for the lady." He gestured at me.

"Oooh!" The woman looked way too excited to see me. "You're a human!"

"Well...yes." I smoothed my hands down my sides.

"I'm Lievoa Kyradus, the owner and the main dress designer of this store. My cousin is married to a human, too. Her bakery shop is right here, in the mall. Did you try any yet?"

"The Earth Girl's Desserts? I love their cupcakes."

"Yes! That's the one. She's not there today, sadly. But she would love to see you. Are you in the group Earth Brides of Voran?"

"No." I had no idea there was such a group.

"Why not? Every human woman I know is in that group. It's so helpful, they say, especially when you're new to the planet."

I would've loved to chat with the friendly woman, but the professor didn't have that much patience.

"How about the pajamas?" he reminded her with a pointed look.

"Oh, yes. This way, please." The woman led us out of the labyrinth of stands filled with pretty dresses and into a section of the store that displayed loungewear and lingerie. "What are you two in the mood for? Naughty or nice?" She swept her arm along the wall display of lingerie ranging from pink and frilly, to bright and see-through, to black and shiny.

"Wow..." I exhaled, taking in all this goodness.

The professor's sharp cheekbones darkened with blush. He cleared his throat. "Something far more practical, please."

"And comfy," I added, then clarified, "We're not married."

The woman's eyebrows rose to the thick curls of fur between her horns. "You're not? Oh, I'm so sorry." Her gaze darted from Professor Thormus to my belly, then back again. Recognition spread on her lively face. "Oh, how so very silly of me!" she exclaimed, grabbing his hand. "You're Professor Kear Umhra Thormus! With Madam Maya Gupta! I should've recognized you two from the newspaper pictures right away. I'm a huge fan of your work."

"Thanks," he muttered, looking around as if searching for a place to hide.

"Please take a seat." She gestured at an armchair in the fitting room area. "I'll have the drone bring you some refreshments. Meanwhile, I'll take care of Madam Maya. You won't have to worry about a thing."

As the professor sat in an armchair, sipping the bitter Voranian tea, Lievoa grabbed a few pajamas and ushered me into a changing room.

Choosing a set of pajamas took me all of two minutes. However, Lievoa didn't stop there. Before I could change back into my pantsuit, she'd stuffed the fitting room with cute maternity dresses, pretty bras, and sexy panties.

"I have shoes, too," she informed me, scowling at my worn hospital flats. "I order quite a few styles for my sister-in-law and her friends from Earth. Well, technically, she's my...what? Cousin-in-law? Since she's married to my cousin? But she really feels like a sister to me. I love her. She's great."

I eyed the colorful treasures she'd hung up all over the fitting room. "But... We just came here for the pajamas."

"Oh, I'm sure Professor Thormus doesn't mind my making you look presentable, do you, Professor?" she called out to him from behind the screen blocking his view of the changing room.

He muttered something into his cup of tea. It could very well be, *"Yes, I fucking do."* But Lievoa chose to interpret it as, *"No, absolutely not. Go ahead, Maya, buy anything this nice lady throws at you and more."*

"See?" She beamed. "Let's start with this dress. I'm dying to see it on you."

After two rather exhausting hours, two more pots of tea for the professor, and his visit to a barber in between, Lievoa and I finally settled on three maternity dresses, two more pairs of cozy pajamas, and some loungewear for me to wear around the hospital without looking like I'd just jumped off the examination table. She also found me a pair of fuzzy slippers and adorable shoes with flower rosettes and cushioned soles that made the shoes feel as comfy as clouds beneath my feet.

I tried the shoes on and didn't want to take them off. They felt so comfy, despite their heels. The cute kitten heels clicked cheerfully on the hard floor of the store when I took a few steps around the room, testing the fit.

"How do you feel?" Lievoa asked, giving me a once-over. "Because you look fantastic."

"The shoes are so comfy!" I gushed. "And the dress... Oh, it's simply gorgeous."

I smoothed my hands down the soft, green fabric of the maternity dress I was wearing. It had see-through sleeves embroidered with tiny flowers, reminding me of spring. I smiled, admiring my reflection in the mirror. I looked pretty, fresh, happy. Glowing.

"Comfy shoes are important for people with feet," Lievoa nodded, tipping her brightly painted horns. "Feet are very delicate. I've learned that from my sister-in-law. She loves the foot massages that my cousin gives her all the time."

"Foot massages are nice," I agreed.

Lievoa swung the screen aside, proudly presenting me to the world, even if the professor was the only one out there right now.

"What do you think, Professor Thormus?"

Dropping his tablet on the magazine table by his chair, he rose to his hooves. His violet eyes traveled from my face down to the cute heels on my feet then back up again, studying me as if he saw me for the first time. His gaze left me warm, a heat wave passing through my body in its wake.

I cleared my throat, fidgeting with the silky material of the dress.

"It's pretty, isn't it?"

"Very," he echoed, taking a step closer.

It felt warmer here than it was inside the fitting room. Or maybe it was because the professor came closer? So close, I could smell his cologne. I never knew he wore any, and maybe he didn't back at the hospital. Was he wearing it just for me today? That was a silly thought, wasn't it?

Lievoa scanned our purchases, using the store drone, then packed them into bags while the professor and I just stood there, staring at each other.

He'd had a fresh trim of his fur and beard while I was in the fitting room. His horns had been shined, too, with a silver spiral of paint added to each. The visit to the barber must have left him smelling this exceptionally good, I realized.

I drew in some air through my nostrils, filling my lungs with his scent. It had a little bit of citrus in it, a little bit of spice, and a whole lot of alien male...

Something fluttered inside my chest then slowly descended into my belly, spreading through my body with a shiver of pleasure.

"I added an extra pair of *pajamas*. A present from me," Lievoa told me with a wink.

The professor yanked his sleeve up to let the drone scan his charge bracelet to pay. Then he turned to me, clearly impatient to get going. I promptly thanked Lievoa for all her help and hurried to the exit with him.

"Thank you," I said as we exited the store and he flagged a mall drone to carry our bags.

"No need to thank me." He shook his head. "The clinic is supposed to provide you with clothes. It's in the contract."

"True, but hospital gowns are clothes, too. There was no obligation for you to buy all this expensive stuff." I pointed with my thumb over my shoulder at the drone whirring behind us with the load of shopping bags.

He flexed his jaw. "It was my oversight not to do it earlier. I should've bought it all on the day of your arrival to Voran."

"But you were too eager to get into my uterus first, weren't you?" I laughed. "You couldn't wait to start the study. I don't think you even thought about me as anything but the research subject until recently."

I said that without accusation. I'd come to Voran to participate in the study. It wasn't the professor's fault we hadn't connected in any other way before. But he seemed flustered by my words.

His eyes dipped to my bare legs under the hem of my mid-thigh-length dress. He jerked his head, flicking his gaze away.

As we passed by yet another storefront, a robot AI greeted him from the doorway, "Good afternoon, Professor Kear Umhra Thormus. Would you like to come in for an unscheduled visit?"

I looked at the name of the store—*Dream Spa.*

"Is that a massage place? One of those with the sex pods?"

The massage spas were often mentioned in Voranian movies and shows. They provided a wide range of body massages, including sexual stimulation. From what I learned, there was no stigma attached to using them in Voran. On the contrary, it was encouraged as a healthy habit for overall wellbeing, especially for men.

With the Voranian population being so heavily skewed toward males, the pods provided a handy solution for an easy release of physical tension, including that of a sexual nature.

The professor's cheeks darkened with blush, however, his eyes shifting as he bit out, "Not today," to the AI screen mounted on a tall stand, then briskly stomped by.

I craned my neck, catching a glimpse of rounded pods deep inside the spa. They looked like a slick version of tanning beds that fully concealed a person inside and reminded me of the massage pods in the hospital. I used those strictly for therapeutic purposes, but now I wondered if those could be configured for sex as well.

If so, the professor could've used them, too. It'd probably be cheaper for him to stay at the clinic. But maybe he preferred to use the pods off site, to separate business from pleasure, so to say.

"We'll see you next weekend then, Professor Thormus," the AI robot chirped behind us.

The professor nodded in acknowledgement but said nothing. He appeared to fully regain his composure now. Whatever that momentary flash of bashfulness was all about, it had passed.

However, *my* thoughts remained on the spa. The weekend was in two days. And now, I imagined the professor lying inside the pod. Naked. Soft rubbery sleeves and firm rollers massaging his large body. The AI sending stimulating images directly into his brain.

Back at the clinic, I'd received leg and foot massages. The atmosphere projected into my brain had been soft music, bubbling brooks, and a breeze whispering in a meadow.

The sex function, I imagined, would have very different settings and imagery.

What would the professor be fantasizing about when he came undone? It wasn't easy to imagine this calm, detached man losing control and panting while covered in sweat. His fur wild and messy, his eyes shut in pleasure, his teeth bared in his chase of the climax...

"Are you hungry?" Professor Thormus asked.

And now I was the one blushing, hiding my eyes from him, as if caught doing something very illicit.

Why on earth would I think about the professor in a sex pod? For all I knew, he might get foot massages there too, just like me... Um. *Hoof* massages. Was there such a thing?

"Sure," I mumbled, quickly shoving the images of him being jerked off in a sex pod out of my head. However, the arousing tingling along my skin continued to simmer warmly.

Where did all that come from?

I'd heard some women had heightened libidos during pregnancy. It hadn't been my case so far. Was this how it started?

On the other hand, I hadn't had sex for a very long time. Pregnant or not, I missed a man's touch.

And now, I was thinking about the professor holding me in his arms as I cried last night. He felt so warm and strong. His arms...

With a tug on my hand, the professor snapped me out of my inappropriate thoughts once again. He led me to one of the indoor gazebos with a tearoom underneath. The glass ceiling over it was lifted, allowing the breeze to flutter through.

"Can I have a dessert?" I asked, forcing my mind to focus on things that didn't involve the professor being naked.

He moved his jaw, twitching his beard.

"Maybe a fruit salad," he conceded. "With a drizzle of tree nectar."

Chapter 11

Kear

"*Hi Walter,*

Thank you so much for your reply. I'm glad you decided to give us time. But that shouldn't mean we should stop writing to each other. Talk to me. Write to me. I want to know how you're doing and what you're thinking about. It'll help me to better understand where your doubts are coming from. Maybe we could mend some things before I come home. There are still so many months left.

I can't wait for this to be over. Being here feels confining, and I'm counting the days until I'm free again."

Maya wasn't happy. That much was clear even to Kear, who read women's bodies like an open map but saw their minds as a confusing, impenetrable jungle. She didn't say she was outright miserable in her letter, but the sadness and loneliness seeped through, clear even as it was subtle.

This wasn't right. It had never been his intention to make her feel trapped and caged in Voran. All he'd ever wanted was to keep his study subject safe in a controlled environment.

That had to change, but there was more that needed to be done.

Maya was a quiet, gentle person. She didn't complain, taking it all until the breaking point. But she deserved so much more in life. Like any woman, she deserved love and support, not a man who would abandon her on an alien planet simply because another woman happened to be closer.

Maya deserved so much better than that asshole.

Sadly, all she had now was Kear.

Standing in the middle of the workroom in his apartment, he kept staring at her letter displayed on the screen of the house drone that hovered in front of him. The foreign words of Maya's mother tongue looked like strings of an unsolved puzzle to him. But their meaning still rang in his mind, echoing his translator implant.

Maya wasn't happy.

She needed reassurance. Some kind words. A letter from the man she loved. The letter that only Kear could write for her now.

The problem was that Kear hadn't written a love letter in his entire life. He'd never received one either. The closest to a love letter he'd ever gotten were the notes of appreciation from his patients. None of which would do in this situation.

"Find a love letter template." He barked at the AI.

"Sorry, the request cannot be completed," came the reply.

It appeared the people on his planet didn't take shortcuts with their romantic communication. Which meant he'd have to write one from scratch.

"Fine. Find some love letter examples, then." He scratched at the base of his horns and amended, "Are there any from Earth?"

As an Earth woman, Maya would respond better to the style of her home planet, he figured.

"The archives of the Liaison Committee now include a collection of books and movies in several languages from Earth," the AI informed him. "Would you like me to pull quotes from works in the romance genre?"

"Yes, please." He had to start somewhere.

He stared at the screen as it filled with strings of text. The screen glowed softly, extending from the shiny disk of the drone.

What did Maya say was the pet she had as a child?

"What is a *dog?*" he asked the AI.

Pictures of four-legged animals appeared on the screen as the drone read the descriptions out loud. The images differed vastly, depending on the breed. But overall, the *dog* creature had a tail and was covered with fur. And it looked nothing like his drone.

He shook his head. Women in general were hard to understand. Maya being a human added an extra layer of enigma for him.

"Alright, let's hear the love quotes," he said to the drone, getting rid of the *dog* pictures.

"I love you against my better judgment," the AI read.

"I love you" was a good start for a love letter, he supposed, but the overall meaning of the sentence seemed rather offensive. It implied the man didn't want to love the woman. That he thought it unwise. Personally, Kear agreed with him—love certainly was an imprudent emotion. But the quote didn't fit with Maya's situation.

He frowned, rubbing his neck. "Is there anything else?"

"I can't live without you."

"Well, that's a blatant lie."

He knew for a fact that no one died from rejection or separation. Every male in his family, other than him, had been rejected by a woman, some many times over.

His mother chose another man over his father, even though they remained friends, and she agreed to carry Kear and his brothers for him. One of Kear's brothers dated a woman for three years before she declined his marriage proposal. The other brother had dated at least ten women in his life. He'd proposed to them all and had been rejected by every one of them.

The odds just weren't in men's favor in Voran. That was the main reason Kear had decided long ago not to even try courting anyone. He was perfectly content with his life, free of heartache. Never in a million years would he have thought he'd need to write a love letter one day.

"Anything else?" He prompted the next quote.

"I'll die for you."

"What?" He barked a laugh.

What good would a man's dying do to the woman he loved? How was his death supposed to make her happy?

"Humans are weird," he muttered under his breath, stomping around the room in circles. "Anything else? Please. There must be something more...*reasonable.*"

"You complete me."

What the fuck was that supposed to mean?

His head hurt, trying to decipher the meaning of this one. It made no sense whatsoever. Something must be lost in translation here.

Frustration filled him with irritation as the AI kept firing quotes at him, all of them weird and useless.

"You are my best friend, my lover, my everything," sounded from the drone, and Kear paused.

Did this one sound promising?

The overall quote was stupid, just like the rest of them. No one was anyone's "everything." People didn't live, eat, and breathe each other. But one word didn't offend his common sense as much as the rest.

Friend.

It didn't sound false when he thought about Maya and her situation. She had been with that man for ten years. That was a long time to spend with anyone. At some point, on some level, she and her asshole boyfriend must've been friends.

More importantly, that was the word Kear could relate to as well. He could think of Maya as his friend when writing to her.

In the three days since their trip to the mall, he hadn't found the time to take her out again, but they had been meeting every day for lunch in the rooftop café. He'd learned more about her life back on Earth and told her more than just bullet notes about his own life.

Maya had become the closest person he currently had to a friend. He had his family, his colleagues, but he couldn't think of any one person he'd be talking to regularly on a daily basis other than her.

"Start a new letter," he commanded the drone. "Dear Maya..."

She would prefer a nickname here. But he couldn't come up with any, and he refused to use that silly *Pooh Bear* moniker, especially, since he got a feeling Maya didn't particularly like that one herself.

Her name would have to do for now.

"Dear Maya. It was a pleasure to hear from you... No. Wait." He rubbed his forehead. This was going to be hard, even if he had any usable love quotes. "Let me think."

A friend. He was writing to a friend who was hurt and needed his support.

"Let's try this 'Dear Maya, I'm very sorry...'"

It was late into the night when the letter was finally finished. He felt more tired than after a complex labor and delivery of a patient.

"All right," he said to the drone, feeling winded, as if after an intense physical workout. His brain hurt. The stomping of his hooves around the room echoed in his ears. But there was an unexpected lightness in his chest. Like he'd done something worthwhile. "Let me hear it."

The drone read out loud.

"Dear Maya,

I'm so, so sorry about that stupid letter I sent you. I think I missed you especially hard that night, feeling particularly lonely, so it all came out wrong and in a most hurtful way. I should've slept on it instead of sending it right away. Things certainly look better now, after I've given it some thought.

You're still not here, and I still miss you, but I cherish the connection we have and don't wish to sever it. You have been my friend for so long. I need you in my life.

Whatever happens, I'm here for you. Yes, please, let's talk. Write to me. Tell me how you're feeling, both physically and emotionally. I want to know everything. Obviously, I have no idea what it's like to be pregnant or what it's like to be alone on an alien planet so far away from home. But I realize it couldn't be easy.

Please remember that I'm here for you, despite the distance. No matter what, you have me to talk about anything that bothers you, and I'll do everything to make it better. Because more than anything in the world, I wish for you to be happy."

Was it good? He didn't have the same confidence he'd felt after writing that first "dry, short" letter. But that might be a good thing, since Maya didn't really like that one.

Writing this one left him feeling somewhat uncomfortable. Maybe because this letter was more personal? He might've used something else than just his brain to come up with this one. The words seemed to have come from deep inside his chest somewhere. And now, he felt oddly vulnerable and unsure.

But did it sound like a love letter?

He didn't explicitly state "I love you" in the letter. It just didn't fit. It sounded false, just like all those love quotes the drone had gathered for him. But maybe he could tuck the word "love" in somehow.

"Sign 'Love, Walter,'" he said to the drone, wincing at the sound of the boyfriend's name. It cut across his hearing like a false note in a song. But it had to be done. He couldn't possibly put his own name there.

Once done, he made the AI read the whole thing to him one more time.

And yes, it did feel more personal. The signature might say "Walter" but these were Kear's words. He meant what he wrote. He wished to be there for Maya. She tried to be strong, dismissing his concerns to his face, but maybe she'd find it easier to express her worries in writing. If he knew exactly what bothered her day to day, it would make it easier for him to help her.

"Change the language and send."

He stared at the drone as the words of the Voranian language morphed into that of the language Maya spoke, then melted away from the screen as the letter was sent.

One phrase from it imprinted into his mind's vision, lingering long after the rest was gone.

"I missed you..."

He rubbed his chest, feeling these words particularly acutely for some reason. An hour at lunch didn't seem like enough time with her.

He hadn't taken Maya to an outdoor park yet. Maybe he could do it this week?

Chapter 12

Maya

"This is *acax* fruit." The professor handed me a long juicy stick curved into a multi-colored spiral. "Not very nutritious," he noted under his breath with a frown, "but it won't hurt as an exception to the rule once in a while."

I giggled at him trying so hard to justify feeding me a treat, then grabbed the curly string out of his hand before he had a chance to change his mind.

"Aw, you're spoiling me, Professor," I teased, biting into the end of the stick. If uncurled, it'd be probably as long as my arm, and it was as thick as my thumb. It felt like rubber in my hand, dangling like a long skinny sausage. But the inside was soft and cool, with a fresh fruity taste. "Oh, it's good. Are you not having any?"

I noticed he only brought one *acax* fruit, and he wasn't going for another one, taking a seat on the park bench next to me instead.

"I don't usually eat those."

"Why not? Not enough nutrients for you?"

"Exactly."

"But you aren't pregnant."

He huffed a laugh. "True."

"And even if you were, you just said there was no harm in eating it once in a while, right?"

"I did," he agreed.

"So." I flicked my wrist, bringing the other end of the spiral closer to him. "Want to take a bite?"

He straightened his back, staring at the fruit.

"Come on. Just a taste." I wiggled it in front of him. "Don't worry, I don't have cooties. Nothing contagious that you can catch by sharing food with me."

"I know *that*," he muttered softly. "I make sure every day that you stay healthy."

He certainly did. By now, Professor Thormus knew my body's inner workings better than I did. Maybe it should feel weird having a stranger that intimately familiar with all aspects of my biology, but after so many months in his care, it felt natural.

He took a bite of my fruit, chewed, and swallowed, not saying a word.

"And?" I stared at his lips that turned glossy with juice.

A drop trembled in the corner of his mouth, and I fought the urge to brush it off with my thumb. The man spent a considerable amount of time between my thighs on a daily basis, but me touching his face seemed inappropriate. I didn't think he'd like being touched.

His tongue darted out, catching the drop. Dark red and tapered at the tip, his tongue unfurled like a ribbon before disappearing into his mouth once again. I knew Voranian tongues were considerably longer than humans', but I hadn't seen one up close like that before.

"What would it feel like while kissing?" a sudden thought popped into my head, and I nearly choked on my fruit stick.

Musing about kissing the professor was the last thing I wished to do. Clearly, such a large break in my sex life must be messing with my head.

"How did you like the fruit?" I jerked the stick in my hand, desperate to distract myself from the sudden turn my thoughts had taken.

"It's nice." He nodded, licking his lips again.

I averted my eyes from his mouth this time. "Why don't you eat it more often, then?"

He shrugged a wide shoulder. "*Acax* fruit is a comfort food. It's sold in public places like parks, zoos, and other attractions for a quick burst of energy and flavor. We don't serve it at the hospital."

"Do you only eat food available at the hospital?"

"That's where I live."

Against my better judgment, I slid my gaze down his muscular frame, barely contained by the pair of beige pants and the lavender shirt he was wearing. Voranians loved bright colors. Both the nature and the people around us burst with vibrant summer hues. For this outing, Professor Thormus had traded his white hospital coveralls for street clothes. Only they still were of subtle colors. I wonder if living in the sterile hospital environment of white and chrome had influenced his preference for muted shades.

"That explains it." I nodded, taking another bite of my *comfort fruit*.

"Explains what?"

"The fact that you don't have an ounce of fat on you and a whole lot of muscles."

He followed my gaze to his thick bicep.

"Taking care of one's physical wellbeing is important. I spend too much time stationary as my work requires. I have to exercise in order to move. It helps to clear my head, too."

"You work out daily?"

"Every morning. In my exercise room." He dropped his gaze. The confidence with which he usually talked about his work left him. Talking about the more private aspects of his life must be something he didn't do very often. "I've been following the same weekly program since I came back from Tragul. It's based on my combat training and includes sparring with a robot."

It didn't surprise me that he used the same program for years. The professor seemed to thrive on routine. It made me appreciate him taking the time from his busy schedule to hang out with me even more.

"I mostly just watch TV for fun," I said. "But when I was growing up, I loved gardening."

"Gardening?" He tilted his head, his eyebrows rising in surprise.

I nodded. "There is true satisfaction in nurturing a plant from a seed. Nothing ever tastes as good as the fruits and veggies that I grew in my little garden." I glanced at him sheepishly, thinking about what I'd just said. "It may not sound like much of an achievement to someone like you—"

"But it is," he disagreed. "I don't think I could grow anything without the help of my AI. My apartment would look like a desert wasteland if it wasn't for the drones maintaining all the plants."

I smiled, but the professor's expression remained serious.

"I'll have more plants brought to your room," he said. "Or better yet, I'll order whatever seeds you want, and you can plant them yourself. Would you like that?"

Excitement warmed my chest at the thought of having something to do. I hadn't had a garden since I left the small town where I grew up to go to college. Then, I moved in with Walter, and we ended up even farther away from my hometown, living in a big city. I hadn't even had a single potted plant at our place. There just hadn't been time to properly look after it.

"I'll try," I replied uncertainly. The luscious Voranian flowers looked like they required specialized care. "I'm not familiar with the plant forms here."

"The hospital drone will help you with any information you need." He gave me a closer look. "Anything else you would like to do while you're here? I know you've been bored, but you don't have to be anymore."

I twisted the remaining fruit string in my fingers.

"You know, back home, staying in and relaxing was a rare treat. Here, that's all I've been doing, to the point that I'm actually looking forward to going out now. These trips feel special." I tilted my face up to the sunshine. A light breeze played with the ends of my unbound hair. The heady scent of summer flowers filled the air along with the chatter of people and the laughter of kids. "It's nice here."

The professor shifted on the bench to face me fully. He blinked, catching my gaze, then grabbed my hand holding the *acax* fruit.

"This does taste good," he said.

Bringing my hand closer, he took another bite of the fruit.

"Hey!" I laughed. "This was supposed to be *my* treat."

Twisting my hand, I bit the fruit from the opposite end.

There wasn't that much of the fruit left. With both of us biting from each end, the professor's mouth moved toward mine.

His eyes ended up right in front of mine. In the bright sunshine, their color lightened to gentle lavender. Startled by his closeness, I sucked in a deep breath through my nose, filling my lungs with air saturated with the sun-heated spice of his skin mixed with the woodsy flavor of his cologne.

If each of us took just another bite of the fruit stick, it'd be gone completely, and we'd be kissing—in the fashion of Lady and the Tramp.

This was wrong.

I jerked away. The short piece left of the fruit fell to the bench between us.

The professor cleared his throat. "I'll get you another one."

"No." I stopped him. "It's okay. I'm not hungry anymore."

Not hungry for *food*.

What on earth was going on with me?

His warm hand covered mine on the bench between us.

I looked up at his face. His eyes darkened to a deeper shade of purple as he slid his gaze down my front, then to our hands on the bench. Of the wild mix of emotions playing out on his face, curiosity seemed to be the predominant one.

He stared at our linked hands in wonder, as if trying to read the feelings the connection brought up in him.

His hand was large, but the palm felt soft, save for a few hard calluses at the base of his fingers, probably from the exercise equipment he used in the mornings. His claws were all filed down to the tips of his fingers for that gentle medical touch of his. Though, the way he was squeezing my hand right now felt far from *medical*. He slid his thumb over my skin, then fitted his fingers between mine, tilting his head to admire them laced together like that—my light-brown and his dark-gray.

He seemed curious. Curious about the way our hands linked like puzzle pieces, so very different yet compatible, nevertheless. He appeared intrigued by the many paths where this one touch could lead us.

I suddenly found myself intrigued, too, as the warmth of his touch spread from my hand to the rest of my body. It swirled in my stomach, making me lightheaded.

Had I ever felt like this before with anyone else?

And more importantly, did I want to go there?

I had a boyfriend. Kind of. Walter hadn't explicitly stated he wanted us to be a couple again, but his latest letters held hope for our relationship.

He sounded different than before. Gone were the silly nicknames he liked giving me. Surprisingly, there were none of his usual complaints, either. He didn't really write anything about himself at all. Instead, his words were saturated with concerns for me.

He sounded mature, supportive, and wishing to solve my problems, instead of just complaining about his.

And maybe Walter had grown in my absence? Maybe living on his own had helped him mature, since he didn't have me around to make sure he had milk for his cereal or a clean shirt for work.

Either way, I felt we might have a chance again. In his letters now, he seemed to hold back a little, not throwing words around just to convince me. Like he was trying to step back and start from a better place this time. And I was all for it.

But if so, there was no place for any "curiosity" or "intrigue" between the handsome Voranian professor and me.

I gently freed my hand from his hold.

"What happened to the paint you had on your horns?" I attempted to ease the charged tension hanging between us by changing the subject.

"The paint?" He lifted his hand to his horns that had been scrubbed free from the silver spirals he'd had painted on during the visit to the barber while I was in the fitting room in Lievoa's store. "Did you like the paint?"

Every Voranian in the park had their horns painted, men and women. Some used glowing neon colors or the reflective glitter paint that made the designs on their horns sparkle and shine as if illuminated.

"It was pretty." I loved the Voranian unapologetic passion for everything loud and bright. The professor's simple spirals had looked rather plain in comparison. But now, even they were gone.

"I had them painted for a special occasion, an event I attended last weekend."

"What event was it? If you don't mind my asking."

"Not at all. It was an assembly of professionals in my field of Interspecies Reproduction. I made a speech. So, I had to look fashionable for the crowd and the pictures." He gave me a shy smile.

He could be so proud and confident about his work and at the same time so insecure and bashful over the paint on his horns.

"What was your speech about?"

He rested his gaze on me. "You."

"Me?"

His eyes flicked down to my middle.

"Oh." I splayed a hand on my belly covered by my dusty-rose maternity dress, one of the three that we'd bought from Lievoa's store. "Right. *Interspecies reproduction.* That would be me, wouldn't it? How did your speech go?"

His face lit up at once, his voice lifting. "Very good. This study is of utmost interest in the scientific community. I wasn't the only one working in this area."

"But you are the only one who succeeded."

"So far. Yes. Though there are at least two other scientists who have come close to breakthroughs of their own."

"No matter what, they can never be first anymore, right? I'm the only one pregnant."

"Well, speed is important, but it's not everything in this case. There is always room for improvement in any method. If theirs turns out to be in any way safer or more efficient..."

His voice trailed off, and I finished for him, "Would it take away from your achievement?"

He drew in a breath, flattening his lips against his teeth. "I try not to look at it that way. At the end of the day, our goal is the same—to give humans and Voranians a safe alternative to the current system."

"Professor Thormus!" suddenly came from right beside us.

A Voranian man nearly tripped, rushing to our bench. He carried a toddler on each arm and one on his shoulders. I jerked my arms up instinctively, ready to catch the children if he fell, but to my relief, he managed to keep his balance.

"Professor Thormus! It's so nice to see you." The man beamed. "Do you remember these little guys?" He bounced the kids in his arms and on his shoulders.

The professor's expression warmed as he took in the little boys.

"Of course I do." He smiled. "Good afternoon, Instructor Zier Ommai Hilgus. How are you?"

"Oh, good, good. Thank you. The boys are doing great in the academy."

All three boys were staring at me, sucking on their thumbs. They had identical lime-green eyes, just like their dad's, and looked like the cutest carbon copies of each other. Their tiny horns were barely an inch long, and their fur seemed so soft, I barely resisted the urge to ask to hold them.

The professor chatted with their father for a little while. Every now and then, Instructor Hilgus would adjust his grip on the kids in his arms or jerk his head away from his son on his shoulders who tried to tickle his face with the arrow tip of his tail. But he seemed to manage the three with exceptional skill and patience.

The professor didn't formally introduce us, there simply was no time. The toddlers stopped staring at me to start bouncing in their dad's arms. They pulled him toward the play structures a short distance from our bench.

After a little chatter, the man said goodbye to the professor and nodded to me, "It was nice seeing you, Madam Maya Gupta. Wishing you a great pregnancy and delivery."

The introduction wasn't necessary, after all. There had been enough news coverage of my pregnancy for people to know who I was.

"Thank you." I smiled and waved goodbye to the children as their dad hauled his brood over to the play area for them to burn off some energy.

"Did you deliver his babies?" I asked the professor after the man had left.

"I did." He nodded. "I met Instructor Hilgus years ago. He taught me how to operate my personal aircraft."

"I thought those things flew by themselves," I quipped.

"They do, once you program and maintain them properly, which Instructor Hilgus taught me how to do. He also taught me how to hand-fly it, just in case. When he decided to start a family, he came to my clinic. The triplets were delivered by a surrogate who chose to remain anonymous. But Instructor Hilgus came for updates regularly. He was in the clinic during the delivery, too."

"How did that work? Since the woman wanted to remain anonymous."

"With anonymous surrogates, the father stays in a different room. The children are then brought to him as soon as they're born. He's the first to hold them, other than the medical staff."

I nodded. That was similar to what my sister-in-law did. She got all the necessary postpartum care while the biological parents held the baby.

Something in my belly twitched, and I splayed my hand over it.

"Just to let you know, I don't mind if the parents come into the delivery room if they so wish."

"You don't?" He stretched his shoulders, looking uneasy.

"No. I would actually love to see them together—the parents and the baby I carried for them. It'd be the perfect conclusion of the study for me to meet the happy family, don't you think?"

He cleared his throat, glancing aside. "Well. It's still a while until the birth."

"I know. Sometimes it feels like forever." I rubbed my belly. "Do you know if the parents have already chosen a name for the baby?"

"They did not," he replied flatly. "How far in advance do humans choose names for their children?"

"Oh, it depends on so many things. For example, I'm not even married yet, but I already know what I want to call my baby if I ever have a girl. Just for a girl, though. I haven't settled on a boy's name yet. But if I have a daughter, I'll name her Anika, like my grandmother. She was a tough, brave woman who moved countries as a widow with three small children in tow. It wasn't easy for her to make a new start like that, but she made it. She raised her kids on her own and lived long enough to see some of her grandchildren get married before she passed away. I often wish to have her strength and determination."

He smiled gently. "Well, in a way you've gone even farther. You've moved planets, not just countries. I'm sure your grandmother would be proud of you."

My all-expense-paid trip wasn't quite the same as my grandmother's ordeal. But I liked knowing that I'd done something none of my family had—I'd visited an alien planet.

"HI WALTER,

Thank you so much for your letters. Somehow, you always manage to say all the right things that I need to hear, making me feel better.

I don't know where all of this will lead at the end. But I love hearing from you. It makes me feel less alone. Mom writes too, of course, whenever she can. But it's not very often. She's very busy with my baby nieces. My brother is working a lot, and his wife is taking night classes. Mom is helping them with the twins. She's there every single day, even on the weekends.

Things got more exciting here in Voran. I make regular trips outside the hospital and not just to go shopping. Though, Voranian fashion is the cutest. You'd never let me wear anything so tacky back home. But here, bright colors are all the rage.

I wonder if the reason for their love of colors is because Voranians are a kind of monochromatic people themselves. They're gray from head to toe...I mean, to hoof. *Everything is gray—their fur, horns, faces. So, they make their homes and clothes as bright as possible to bring color into their lives. I love it about them.*

The hospital is rather subdued in terms of color, though. For hygienic reasons, it has no flowers in most rooms. Only in some hallways, the atrium, and the roof terrace.

But once you step out, the world looks like a Pixar movie.

I've been to two different shopping malls and several outdoor parks. The weather is great—warm and sunny. The flowers started blooming almost as soon as the snow melted. And now, the summer is in full swing.

Maybe that's why my mood has improved, too. Winter is often depressing everywhere.

It helps that I now have company more often, too. Professor Thormus, the head of this study, is the one who takes me out. He's such a nice person. Smart and kind. Everyone loves him. People literally come to him on the streets all the time to thank him for his work, and he generously offers help. He's a brilliant doctor. With him, I'm in good hands.

How are you, Walter? How is the store doing? I assume it's okay since you never write to me about the store anymore. It must be a good thing because most of what you wrote before was about your fighting with the staff. I hope you guys found common ground and learned to work together.

What are you doing in your free time? I'm sorry I'm not there, and I hope you aren't too bored going places alone.

Write to me about everything and keep writing as often as you can. I love getting letters from you."

Chapter 13

Maya

"**D**ear Maya,
    I'm so glad you're feeling better. It makes me truly happy that you're enjoying your time in Voran.

You have to take care of yourself. It hurts me that I'm not there to help you more, but please let your professor know if you need anything at all.

I doubt he's as nice a person as you write he is. I've noticed you tend to see the best in people. But it is his job to look after you and provide you with whatever you need while you're in his care. Sadly, he doesn't always seem to know what's best for you. I suspect he doesn't spend much time socializing with people. So please, don't hesitate to tell him what you need.

I'm glad to hear you like Voran. It is a lovely country, from what I know. Just make sure not to overexert yourself. The study is nearing its end. You've done so well. I'm very proud of you, Maya. I really am.

Sorry I didn't realize before how difficult it must be for someone in your situation. My work had been my priority for so long, I failed to consider the toll that being away from home would take on you. I should've been there for you much sooner.

Well, I am here now. And I'll be here for as long as you need me. I've hardly interacted with anyone this frequently before. It's unusual to do so now, but not unpleasant. I often find myself talking to you in my head as I go about my day. I'd tell you about the daily challenges of my work or about the people I meet, then wonder what your reply would be.

It's a very bizarre feeling, Maya, like I always have you with me, and I'm never alone.

I'm afraid I'm getting used to having you in my life and will miss you immensely when you leave... I mean, if we were ever to part from each other.

The work is doing great. Thank you so much for asking. It's busy and very demanding, but also rewarding. I've been working late almost every night for over a month now. But the results are delightful..."

A smile played on my lips as I read yet another letter from Walter, sitting at my usual table in the rooftop garden café.

His letters were a little shorter than before, but he wrote so much more frequently. Sometimes, it would be just a short note with wishes for a good day and reminders to take care of myself. But I got at least something from him every morning.

I liked turning on my tablet, looking forward to yet another message from him. Reading them always put me in a good mood, making it the best way to start the day.

I enjoyed watching changes in Walter. He'd grown more responsible. Even the style of his writing had evolved. He sounded more mature and caring.

His earlier letters had often contained long lists of grievances against everyone and everything, from the weather, to the economy, to every single person who had wronged him since he'd written to me last. It had made him sound rather self-centered. I'd even begun to wonder if being away from Walter gave me a chance to learn things about him I hadn't paid attention to when we lived together, the things I wasn't sure I liked very much.

This new side of him delighted me now. I loved the caring, mature Walter. I believed we were connecting on a deeper emotional level, too. I felt closer to him now than I had when I was back on Earth.

The physical aspect of our relationship had been put on hold, however. Walter hadn't sent me any sexy pictures or videos of himself lately. He didn't even write anything light or flirty anymore.

It was fine for now. We could always rekindle the steamy parts later, couldn't we?

"Would you mind if I joined you, Madam Maya Gupta?" a male voice sounded above me.

I was waiting for Professor Thormus to have lunch together as we did almost daily for the past two and a half months. The Voranian man standing over me wasn't him, though he, too, was wearing a white lab coverall.

His dark orange eyes squinted at me as he smiled. "I've been dying to meet you."

"You have?" I was certain I'd never seen this man in my life. "Why?"

"I appreciate what you're doing for my nation, Madam Maya. This study is phenomenal." He offered me his hand. "I'm Professor Fizier Sussil Egus."

A professor, after all. Just not the one I was expecting.

"Thank you." I placed my right hand on top of his and he covered it with his other one in a Voranian greeting. "But the study belongs to Professor Thormus. My role in it is minimal."

"He would've never been able to achieve what he did without you."

"I guess," I conceded, putting away my tablet. "I'm waiting for him right now, actually."

"Were you planning to have lunch together?"

"Yes. I'm a little early today, but he should be here any minute now. I'm sure he wouldn't mind if you joined us." I gestured at one of the spare chairs at the table.

"I wouldn't be so sure." He smirked but took the seat next to me, then ordered us both tea through a hospital drone.

I stirred the tea in my cup when the deep voice of Professor Thormus boomed over my shoulder.

"Egus? What are *you* doing here?" He glared at our new lunch buddy, visibly annoyed.

His frown didn't stop the rush of excitement through my chest at the sound of his voice or the warm wave of tingling along my skin at the sight of him.

This was the most inconvenient side effect I had developed while spending time with him. As my emotional relationship with Walter was being repaired, physically I was drawn to the professor in a way that grew more and more alarming.

The other man reclined in his chair, clearly not intimidated by the gruff greeting. "Nice seeing you, too, Thormus."

The professor, *my* professor, since there were two of them here now, folded his arms across his chest, his scowl deepening despite the open smile of his colleague.

"I asked what the fuck are you doing here?"

Professor Egus lifted both hands in a pacifying gesture. "I had business with someone at the hospital and came up here to get some food. Then, I spotted the lovely Madam Maya Gupta. And since you've never bothered to introduce us, I took the liberty—"

"You shouldn't have," Professor Thormus cut him off. "Now take your food and leave."

"But Madam Maya and I have just met." Professor Egus pouted. "We've had no chance to have a proper conversation."

"Good. She's heard none of your nonsense yet, then. Now go."

I kept moving my gaze from one man to the other, wondering what got my reserved, even-tempered professor so irritated. Egus seemed friendly and easy-going—a fun lunch companion. I didn't mind him staying. However, not knowing their history, I didn't want to interfere.

"This rooftop terrace is not a part of your clinic, Thormus. I'll stay here for as long as I wish. If Maya doesn't object."

And just like that, Professor Egus ended my neutrality, dragging me into their argument. They both stared at me now, awaiting my decision.

"I... I don't mind," I said, then noticed that Professor Thormus's expression darkened. "Unless of course, there is a reason why you shouldn't be here?"

"There are plenty of reasons," Professor Thormus snapped.

"All of them are only due to your intolerable disposition and grumpy nature," Egus objected with a charming smile. "Lighten up, Thormus. Sit down and have lunch with us. Can't you see you're upsetting our lovely Madam Maya by being your usual cranky self?"

Egus obviously knew what buttons of Kear's to push. My professor shot me a concerned look.

"I'm fine," I assured him.

He nodded, making a visible effort to collect himself, then took a seat on my right. His frown eased somewhat, but the thumb on his right hand placed on the table tapped slightly in a nervous gesture.

It reminded me of the way he tapped on the inside of my knee during the medical exam that morning when prompting me to open my legs wider for him. My heart skipped at the memory, and my inner muscles clenched.

His actual touch was rare, even during an examination. He used medical devices fitted with probes, tips, and scanners that minimized any form of physical contact between us. He also wore gloves during the exams, which made skin-to-skin touch impossible.

Not that I wished for any skin-to-skin contact with Professor Thormus, of course. It'd be all kinds of inappropriate if I did.

This intense attraction must be the result of being alone for too long. I was severely touch-starved by now.

Back on Earth, I'd had a large extended family who loved to hug, a few friends who didn't shy from showing and receiving affection, and a boyfriend who might not be the greatest at sex but who definitely liked having it often.

No wonder I felt deprived of all of it here on Neron. With Professor Thormus being my main companion lately, it seemed both my mind and my body decided to project my longing for physical contact onto him. That had to be the explanation of my physical pull toward him.

The tension at the table grew uncomfortable. To ease it, I took it upon myself to start a conversation.

"So, you don't work at the hospital, Professor Egus?"

"No. I have my own clinic on the other side of the city. It's a happy coincidence that I've run into you. I don't come to this side of town often." He glared at Professor Thormus over the rim of his cup, but his smile remained unchanged when he set the cup down.

I glanced at my professor, too. "How do you know each other if not through work?"

"We went to the same academy," Egus explained, not giving Kear a chance to say a word. "We also work in the same field now. But we only get to see each other a few times a year, at the assembly. Your progress is a major point on the agenda of those meetings now. But it's a shame we have yet to see you there."

"I don't think I've ever been invited." I looked at Professor Thormus for confirmation, but he wouldn't meet my eyes.

He'd always been extremely protective of me, sometimes overly so. It wouldn't surprise me if he didn't forward the invite in his effort to shield me from unnecessary attention.

"Of course you have," Egus exclaimed. "You're always invited. You are our main attraction, so to say. The only reason none of us have seen you yet is because Thormus has been hiding you so diligently. It's such a lucky coincidence that I've met you today."

The more he repeated the word "coincidence" the less I believed it had been. I wouldn't put it past him not to come up here specifically to find me.

"We're all following your progress with bated breaths," Egus continued. "You're a true celebrity in our circles, Maya. It's such an honor to finally meet you in person. I can't wait to brag about it at our next assembly."

"When is the next assembly?"

"In about four weeks." Professor Egus perked up as if at an idea entering his mind. "If you're interested in attending, I'll be honored to bring you as my guest."

"No!" Professor Thormus's voice came out a little too high and a little too loud for the situation.

"I beg your pardon, Professor, but that is up to Maya to decide." Egus turned to me. "Would you like to attend with me?"

"She wouldn't," Professor Thormus replied for me quickly.

But Egus kept looking at me, waiting for my answer.

I lifted a shoulder, uncertain. "Well, I'm not sure I'll fit in… I'm not a scientist."

"The formal presentation can be boring sometimes," Egus agreed. "But it's fairly short. It's followed by a gala with a nice dinner and dance. It'll be fun."

It did sound fun. The introvert in me wished to stay in the familiar safety of the hospital. However, the somewhat more outgoing part of me welcomed the idea of going out. I hadn't been to a party in years. A chance to attend one on Neron before I returned to Earth at the end of the study was just too tempting.

"I—"

The right eye of Professor Thormus ticked as he must've already guessed my answer.

"She'll come with me," he said gruffly.

Professor Egus made a face. "But I invited her first."

"She was invited by the assembly. And she will be attending it. With *me*."

The stormy eyes of Professor Thormus held an equally intense stare of Professor Egus. If glares could spark a fire, we'd be sitting in the middle of an inferno right now. Unsure whether to feel flattered or disturbed by the men fighting over me, I couldn't deny the excitement sparkling inside me.

I turned to Professor Thormus. "Will you really let me go to the gala?"

"If everything is well in four weeks, yes. I will take you to the assembly," he promised.

I was going to a party!

Chapter 14

Maya

"*Hi Walter,*
Guess what happened yesterday? I got invited to a gala tak-ing place in four weeks. It's a fancy event by the sound of it. Professor Thor-mus promised to take me if things continued to go well. No idea what I should wear. What will I even look like by then?"

I put my tablet down on my lap, staring at the garlands of flowers suspended from the ceiling. I designed this planter fixture myself and seeded it with the plants that Kear, or Professor Thormus, had ordered for me.

The delicate golden buds of the flowers hadn't opened yet, but the frilly edges of the petals had curled out already, signaling that the flow-ers would be in full bloom soon. The sight of the healthy, purple gar-lands with golden-yellow buds filled me with pride since I've been dot-ing on these plants for weeks.

I returned my attention to the letter I was writing.

Until our unfortunate but thankfully brief break-up, Walter had never mentioned my pregnancy. I got a feeling he either didn't know what to say to me about it or just didn't want to talk about it. Which was fine, it wasn't about us starting a family anyway. What I was going through this time didn't need to be our mutual experience.

Walter hadn't even seen me pregnant. When I first came to Voran, I sent him lots of pictures of the spaceport, of the city I saw from the air-craft on my way to the hospital, and of the hospital itself. But I'd hardly sent him any pictures of myself, other than a few selfies.

Direct video communication wasn't allowed in my contract. The reasons for that, I'd been told, included the technical limitations of video transmissions between Earth and Neron, time delays, and security concerns. Though, we were allowed to exchange pre-recorded videos that could be scanned by AI before delivery to the recipient.

He had sent me a few sexy videos of himself shortly after my coming to Neron. So that I didn't forget how good he looked naked, he'd said. Until the past few months, he'd asked me repeatedly to send one of me, too. This would be the closest we could get to having "phone sex" during our long-distance relationship.

With my hormones kicking into overdrive as of late, I'd considered making a video for him. However, as my belly grew, I felt less and less confident about my appearance. I feared he just wouldn't find me sexy.

"By the time of the gala, I'll probably be the size of a whale. I won't need a dress but a parachute. Or a tent."

Humor was the way to go about the situation. If I couldn't let a man swoon, hopefully, I could still make him smile.

Chapter 15

Kear

"*Oh my dearest Maya,*

You really have no idea how beautiful you are. It must be my fault. Clearly, I haven't told you enough how attractive I find you.

You have the darkest eyes I've ever seen. They draw me in like the night sky. And just like the sky, they make me feel like I'm flying if I look deep into them.

I adore your smile. Do you know you have the cutest pair of dimples, but they can be seen only when you laugh? I find myself trying to make you laugh just to see them. Though, let's face it, I'm not the funniest person out there. Making you laugh is hard work. But seeing those dimples come out is the best reward ever.

Don't worry about the dress, my Maya, whatever it ends up being. No dress can spoil your beauty. I've seen you try on many different clothes, and you look simply stunning in all of them.

You're such a warm, kind person. And your body... Well, I'd better not write about your body because just thinking about it fills my head with extremely inappropriate thoughts.

How can you even consider that pregnancy would spoil it in any way?

You're carrying a new being inside you. One day soon, it'll be a person who will forever trace the beginning of their existence to you. They may never remember meeting you, but they will never forget what you did for them.

The more I get to know you, Maya, the more I appreciate you. You were like a closed bud of a flower at first, but every letter exchanged between us is like a petal opening to reveal just another part of you. I don't always know what I'll find opening each and every one of them, but I'm looking forward to learning everything there is to know about you.

This, by far, has been the most extraordinary part of my life. And it's all because of you. Whatever happens, I'll be forever grateful for all your letters.

You are an amazing woman, my Maya. You deserve to be loved. Don't ever let anyone make you doubt that."

The drone paused reading, waiting for his instructions. Kear stopped pacing in the middle of his workroom and stared out through the window into the evening sky, the words of the letter echoing in his ears.

Did he really just write all of that?

When did it happen? How did he end up finding all these words? And even more astonishing was that every word made perfect sense to him. Because he *felt* them all. He no longer needed to search for romantic quotes. When it came to Maya, the words just poured out of him.

He gestured for the drone to proceed.

"Your body is beautiful in any dress. I'd give everything just to touch you, my flower.

Miss you."

My flower...

The image of Maya in her green summer dress rose in his mind. And there it was, the nickname he'd been searching for. She truly was like a summer flower—vibrant, warm, and beautiful.

Not everyone could see her in bloom, though. Maya didn't open up just to anyone. But what an amazing feeling it was to have her open up to *him*.

When he wrote to Maya, his brain stepped back, and his heart spoke. His chest felt warm when he finished, his entire body buzzed. He felt like either punching or kissing someone.

Restless energy urged him to move. He turned toward his exercise room despite the late hour. He preferred to exercise in the morning.

But his established routine had been going off the rails lately. And he had no one to blame but the gorgeous pregnant woman with dark, alluring eyes.

His flower...

Fuck. What was he supposed to do when she inevitably left at the end of the study? The thought stabbed him like a knife, and he shook his head, chasing it away. There was still at least a month and a half until the birth of the baby. After that, if she wished, she could stay in Voran for one month longer as per the contract.

"Change the language and send," he ordered the drone.

As the letter disappeared from the screen, a reminder pinged. Today was the night of his appointment at the spa. He'd skipped the one last week, after adjusting his schedule to spend more time with Maya.

But denying himself physical gratification last week could be the reason for his restlessness now.

Determined to keep tonight's appointment, he headed out to his aircraft.

STRETCHING INSIDE THE pod, Kear relaxed his spine and let the machines massage tension and weariness out of his muscles.

Weeks had been flying by fast and yet not fast enough. Every day brought his study closer to completion. It also brought him closer to losing Maya. And he couldn't think of any way to extend her stay in Voran beyond her contract.

Now that he had stepped in for her heartless boyfriend, she believed her relationship was well on track again, and she was eager to reunite with the bastard who wished to have nothing to do with her.

The man must be blind not to see what he was giving up in Maya. He must also be dumb like a hoof if he didn't try to do everything possible and beyond to keep her.

A machine attachment caressed his cock, spreading a pleasant sensation through his body. The massage pod could conjure realistic images in his mind if he so wished. Some people preferred relaxing videos of beaches and colorful valleys. Others enjoyed more exciting visions of people making love to them.

Kear rarely used either. To him, sex was a physical function. The pod worked every part of his body, helping him relax. Why not let it work on his cock, too?

He arched his back, letting the arousal build in anticipation of a speedy climax.

"May we suggest a more suitable setting?" the pod's AI sounded in his brain. *"To make today's session more enjoyable?"*

Maya's face suddenly appeared behind his closed eyelids. The AI had sifted through his memories and fished her face out as a suggestion.

Fantasizing about her in a heightened state of arousal was a bad idea. His cock disagreed, however, swelling harder with a powerful jolt of lust at the sight of her sweet smile.

"Hello, Professor," the machine-conjured Maya murmured, leaning over him.

The swell of her belly rested against his abs. The fragrant, black curtain of her hair draped over them, bringing them closer.

He inhaled, savoring her scent. Deep inside, he knew all of it was just an illusion. AI manipulated his mind using the memories stored in his brain. He marveled, however, at how detailed those images were. Had he collected and stored so many details about her?

Her dark eyes, framed with the thick black eyelashes, held the same expression she often had when looking at him—shy but playful. She held herself back in his presence. Only through her letters had he been getting the full picture of the person she really was.

"Mmm," her image moaned, raking her little fingers through the thick fur on his chest. "Let me make you feel good, Professor."

He couldn't take his eyes off her mouth as her full lips wrapped around his title in the most enticing way.

"Kear," he croaked. "Call me Kear, please."

"As you wish, *Kear*." She leaned closer, her hand sliding down his front toward his crotch.

The most exquisite pleasure rippled along his skin at the sound of his name. He hadn't known how much he wished to hear it from her lips until now.

"Wait." He stopped her from touching his erection. "Wait, please..."

He had to get out of this machine.

Dreaming of having sex with Maya in the pod had not been his intention when he got here.

It carried no violation of laws or even ethics in Voranian society. Women often felt flattered to star in men's sex pod fantasies. The problem was, he feared, the fantasy might spill into reality in this case. He couldn't allow his mind to think about Maya this way. He certainly couldn't build any association between her and his weekly visits to the pod.

She was the subject of his study, his patient. That was the only way he could think about her.

Yet, he couldn't let her go. Even if it was just an illusion.

"Tell me about your day," he said to his own surprise.

What the fuck was he doing?

He had to leave.

"What would you like to know?" She tilted her head in the way he'd seen real Maya do when asking a question.

"Come here." He opened his arm, coaxing her to lie against his side.

The slight weight of her head pressed against his shoulder. His side warmed with the heat generated by the massage pod to replicate her body heat. It felt so real. It looked real too, as Maya's large brown eyes gazed at him.

"Why don't you tell me about your day instead, Kear? What did you do today?"

"Work," he sighed. "It's getting more intense, the closer to the due date we get. The slightest mistake could be devastating now."

"It'll be just fine." She looked serene.

The real Maya wouldn't be this relaxed. She'd be much more involved when talking about the topic. But she would also try to hide her worries and would do her best to comfort him.

She stroked his chest, tangling her fingers in his fur.

"You're so tense, Kear," she cooed, and suddenly he regretted asking her to call him by his name.

It broke the illusion. Maya only ever called him "Professor" or "Professor Thormus." Did she ever think about him as anyone else but the head of research? Did she think about him at all when they weren't together? Did she ever use his first name at least in her mind?

"Your time is up, Professor Kear Umhra Thormus," the mechanical voice of the AI announced in his mind. *"Would you like to extend the session?"*

His cock remained as hard as ever. He was still aching and in need. He should at least let the machine take care of his erection, lest he walk out of the spa looking like he was smuggling a log in his pants.

Though he already knew even if the pod made him come, it would not be satisfying. Nothing the machine could do for him would.

"No," he said, fighting the sting of sadness as the image of Maya melted away. Emptiness replaced the sensation of her lying at his side.

Chapter 16

Maya

"**D**arling, I love your letters so much. Getting them is like being greeted by a warm splash of sunshine in the morning, like getting a hug. After reading them, I feel ready to take on anything the day may bring.

Today was a good day, though.

Professor Thormus took me to an outdoor museum. Actually, it is indoors through the winter, covered by a giant glass semi-sphere. The glass is lifted for the summer, so we could get some fresh air while walking around among the exhibits. I'm sending you as many pictures as the system would let me. Even though the pictures don't do it justice.

I never thought I'd be able to move around this much at almost eight months pregnant. But I've been doing pretty good. Thanks to the professor and his team in large part, of course.

The professor has always been exceptionally protective of me, for obvious reasons. It felt restrictive at the beginning. But now, it doesn't bother me at all. Probably because he's been acting more as a close friend now than a boss. I really enjoy his company.

He knows so much about every single exhibit in the museum. We didn't even need a drone guide for our tour.

The professor doesn't talk much. Even some of the people on his research team told me they find him gruff and unsociable. But really, he's just shy. He isn't good at small talk, but he's amazing at talking about topics that interest him. And with me, he is very talkative and kind. He's my best friend here in Voran..."

I put my tablet down in my lap. The images from our trip to the museum played in a silent slideshow on the opaque TV screen in my apartment. Most pictures were of the exhibits. But I managed to catch Professor Thormus in a few shots.

On one, his back was to me as he was buying a half-open flower from a sidewalk gallery. He had given it to me a moment later, with a shy smile.

"It's at its most beautiful when in full bloom, but it only opens fully under the right conditions," he'd said. Then added softly, "It reminds me of you."

I glanced at the flower that was sitting in a glass pot on the table now. Butterflies fluttered in my stomach, spreading a warm, tingling sensation through the rest of my body.

"My best friend."

The words from my letter bounced in my head with some dissonance. The description I gave of the professor wasn't accurate. The feelings I had for him weren't just "friendly."

The image of him running a hand through the fur between his horns came up next, and I paused the slideshow. He didn't know I took this picture as he had glanced away. He looked so himself in it, his wide shoulders relaxed, a tiny smile playing on his lips.

With their hooves, horns, and fur, Voranians looked so different from humans, many on Earth thought them unattractive. I found Professor Thormus extremely handsome, however. Just looking at his picture made my heart flutter and my knees weak.

His physical power and intelligent confidence, combined with that awkwardly shy streak of his, made for an irresistible combination.

Still, I had to resist whatever drew me to him.

The physical pull was easy to explain. I hadn't had sex in ages, and the professor was a man. A tall, strong, manly man with those violet eyes that sparkled so beautifully in the summer sunshine...

All those pregnancy hormones that some said were supposed to make me feel horny must be raging by now. I had to find a way to rein them in.

What would the professor say if I asked him for a vibrator?

A barrage of images of him using it as a medical probe on me suddenly rushed into my head, robbing me of breath.

I gripped the tablet in my lap, closing my eyes. The right thing to do was to banish these images from my head once and for all. But the warm sensation rushing through my body felt too good to stop it.

My shoulders moved with a slight shiver as the forbidden fantasy played in my mind.

"Open for me, Maya," the professor rumbled in that deep voice of his and tapped the inside of my knee with his thumb. A slim medical probe in his other hand vibrated softly. "Let me take care of you, sweetheart. Let me make you feel good."

The professor's constant concern for my wellbeing made it easy to envision him taking care of *all* my needs, including those that throbbed so urgently between my legs.

This was wrong...

Despite my best efforts, however, Professor Thormus refused to leave my obviously very disturbed imagination.

"Let me touch you." He snapped his gloves off, then slid his large hands down my inner thighs. "Let me taste you..."

His impossibly long tongue snaked out of his mouth, unfurling towards my clit with determination.

Oh God... I snapped my eyes open and jumped off the couch, shoving my tablet aside.

Full-blown desire rushed through my body like a heatwave. My nipples tingled. My inner muscles clenched, wetting my panties. Need throbbed low in my belly with an ache and pressure, begging for release.

I could no longer focus on finishing the letter. God knew what inappropriate things I'd write if I tried...

But then again, maybe Walter wouldn't mind the inappropriate? He used to ask me for sexy videos before. His latest letters had been filled with subtle longing that resonated with me even more deeply.

He missed me. Our sex life might've stagnated a little after ten years of being together. Maybe it was never that explosive to begin with, either. But being apart must've made him realize that what we had was worth preserving.

Maybe what I needed was to see his face again? It'd been a while since he sent me any pictures. Video calls weren't possible between us, but sending videos was allowed.

I hadn't sent him any, thinking he wouldn't like seeing me with my growing pregnant belly. But the loving, reverent tone of his letters of late made me feel far more desirable.

Desire buzzed through me, heating my body. Making a sexy video for Walter would re-direct it toward the right person. Wouldn't it?

All off-planet messages were scanned by the Liaison Committee's AI system before being sent. My video wouldn't contain anything illegal for it to be flagged. But even if it happened, I would mark it private. That way, a live representative would not review it without notifying me first. In which case, I would just tell them what it contained and delete it. No one would see it but Kear.

Walter.

Of course I meant Walter.

God, what was wrong with me? I had to stop thinking all those sexy thoughts about the professor and start fantasizing about my actual boyfriend. I'd think about him while making the video. It didn't have to be long or dirty, just a quick, flirty video. I even had just the right outfit for it.

I rushed to my closet behind a lattice draped with vines and pulled out a bag with the lingerie set from Lievoa's store. The sassy owner had slipped it in with our purchases. It still had the round scanning tags attached, since I'd had no chance to wear it.

After stripping from my comfy pajamas and the maternity underwear, I slipped the lacy panties on. They fit only under my belly, of course, but that was fine. The delicate material caressed my skin in a most sensual way.

The crotch of the panties was constructed from interwoven ribbons that were easily parted in whatever way one pleased to fit through someone's fingers or...other appendages.

I heaved a breath, imagining a long, red tongue snaking through between the ribbons as the man's vivid violet eyes gazed at me from between my parted legs.

Dammit...

Wrong tongue. Wrong eyes. This wasn't the man I should be envisioning right now.

I yanked the cute little top out of the bag next and put it on. Tiny, multi-colored flowers decorated its shoulder straps and neckline. Pregnancy had expanded my chest slightly, too, not just my belly. The ribbons woven into the bra cups stretched around my breasts, lifting them enticingly. My hardened nipples poked out from between the weave.

I had no idea what I looked like, but dressed in this outfit, I sure *felt* sexy.

Padding back into the living room, I found my discarded tablet and turned the video function on. Using the screen as a mirror, I scrutinized my body dressed in the sexy, shamelessly bright pink outfit.

It was probably not something I'd wear on Earth. My friends might find the flowers tacky, and Walter... I honestly wasn't sure what Walter would say about it. When I thought about us being together in bed, I imagined he'd tease me about the ribbons and the lace. But when I remembered the words from his letters, I didn't think he'd care what I was wearing, as long as it made me happy.

And this outfit did make me feel happy and flirty. I smiled, smoothing the frills of the baby-doll top.

Taking a deep breath, I pushed the "record" button.

"Well." I smiled at the camera, running my fingers through my hair to release it from the hairband. "Hi, Kear—"

Shit. Not again.

Why did I say that?

Wrong name. Wrong man.

My cheeks flared with heat from mortification.

Focus, Maya.

Shaking my head, I stopped the video, deleted it, then started the recording anew.

Chapter 17

Kear

He made the drone read his speech out loud one more time. It needed some work. A few charts were missing, along with some points he wished to expand on once he had more data. But overall, it was good. Almost ready for the next assembly that was taking place in a week.

Stepping away from the drone, he plopped onto a couch in his living room. His back ached from hovering over the screens all day. His shoulders felt stiff. He rolled his head, stretching his neck.

These long work hours of late weren't good on his body. His mind didn't get much rest either, as work cut more and more into his sleep.

He skipped the visit to the spa this week again since the latest visit brought him no physical release anyway. Maybe that was where some of his muscle tension stemmed from? He needed a massage and a good night's sleep.

Instead of heading either to the spa or the bed, however, he ordered the AI drone to move closer.

"Notifications on."

He'd had them muted while trying to catch up on work. A wave of sounds came rushing in now, with an ever-increasing number of new messages displayed on the screen—more work.

One name stood out from the long list of people vying for his time and attention—Maya Gupta. That was the only name he was glad to see at any hour of day or night.

Something inside his stomach fluttered with anticipation when he ordered the drone, "Open and read."

"Hi Sunshine," the drone translated. *"I miss you more than ever. I wish you were here. But since you're not, I thought I'd send you something to remember me by until we're together again.*

I'm a little nervous. A lot, actually. But I think it's important for us to remember what we are for each other. Just promise me if you don't totally love what you see in the first few frames, close it and delete the entire thing right away."

Weird. What did she mean by all of this?

A black square of a video attachment sat at the bottom of the message.

"Private," the text read right above it. *"For Kear's eyes only."*

His?

Maya sent it for *him?* Not that Walter guy from Earth?

Did she know Kear was the one writing her letters for over three months now?

Come to think of it, she hadn't mentioned Walter's name in any of her latest letters. She'd referred to him as "darling or "sunshine." Most of what she wrote was about Kear and their time together. And she'd said so many nice things about him.

Relief flooded through him. Lying to her all this time hadn't sat well with him. He didn't regret their correspondence and the obvious positive effect it'd had on her. But he wished he could do it under his own name, not under that stupid moniker, Walter.

But how did she know? And why had she never confronted him about it? Never even mentioned anything about his deception?

Maybe the video had some answers? Maybe it was her way of confronting him now.

"Play," he ordered.

"This video will play just once," Maya's voice sounded as the video square grew, filling the screen. "It will then auto-delete. So, please make sure you're comfortable, darling." Her voice dropped with a sultry note. "And *alone.*"

Alone?

He glanced around, knowing perfectly well that there was no one else but him and the drone in his entire suite.

The video image came into focus.

Maya sat on the small round couch in her apartment here at the hospital. The milky glow from the screen cast pale highlights on her smooth brown skin, and there was *a lot* of her skin on display. Her legs bent, she leaned on a cushion sideways, wearing...

What the fuck was Maya wearing?

He stood up to take a better look. He'd never seen anything like this on her before. Pink, and frothy, and scandalously revealing.

"Okay, so..." She smoothed the see-through fabric over the rounded swell of her belly. "Like I said, if you don't like what you're seeing, please close and delete this right now."

How could any man alive not like what he saw?

He devoured every curve of her body with his eyes, afraid to breathe lest he miss a thing. He had no idea why she sent this to him. But there was no way he could close the video or even force his eyes away from the screen.

"I miss you..." she said softly. "And the truth is, I really, really miss being touched. Can I just pretend this is *your* hand, not mine?"

Lifting a hand, she stroked the side of her neck with the tips of her fingers. His own fingers twitched even as his arms remained stretched down his sides.

He stopped questioning what was going on, completely swept away in the action.

"Do you like the lingerie?" she murmured from the screen.

"Love it," he croaked, forgetting she wouldn't hear him.

"It's rather naughty, isn't it?" She cupped her breast through the fabric.

As her hand slid down a little, he noticed the cups of her top were made from thin, interwoven ribbons. They parted under her squeeze, letting the hard, brown nipple poke through. She flicked it with her thumb, and he nearly choked on his drool.

His knees gave in and he dropped his ass on the couch that luckily happened to be right there. If it wasn't, he'd hit the floor, but it wouldn't really matter. He didn't think he'd notice even if all seventy-six floors of the building collapsed under him. His eyes glued to the screen, all he saw, all he could think about was her.

She sat up, cupping both breasts now. Her eyelids fluttered a little and her mouth parted as she played with her nipples, tormenting him with every squeeze, pat, and tweak.

He dug his fingers into the soft leather of the couch. His blood heated. His heart pounded so hard, he feared it would jump out of his throat and drop to his hooves. He ripped his shirt off over his head. The material tangled in his horns, and he tore at it, getting rid of the shirt without taking his eyes off Maya.

"Oh, it feels so good," she moaned, shifting to open her legs a little.

He jerked his legs wider, too, giving more space to his raging erection. When did he get hard? He had no idea. But his cock throbbed like a metal rod stuck into a burning furnace.

"I wish you could touch me here." Maya slid her hand under her flimsy excuse for a shirt. The muscles in her thighs twitched and another soft moan escaped her lips.

"I wish I could touch you everywhere, sweetheart," he rumbled, tearing his pants open.

His cock sprang into his hand, hot and needy. He would never make it to the spa in time to take care of this. Besides, no machine would be able to replicate what was playing out on the screen for him.

Fuck the sex pods.

Maya glanced at him, her dark eyes twinkling enticingly from under her long, thick eyelashes.

"Do you want to see?" She bit her lip, working her hand between her thighs under her shirt.

"Fuck. Yes." He fisted his cock, gasping in a wave of pleasure and ache. "Show it to me, Maya."

Her eyes held his from beyond the screen as she slowly raised her knees, then parted them, lifting the hem of her lingerie. Her underwear was made of ribbons, too. And they were soaked, her arousal turning the fabric from pink to burgundy.

"Fuuuuck," he growled, flexing his fist around his cock so hard, the pain made him howl. But there was pleasure, too. So, so much pleasure. Watching her touch herself almost made him come right then and there.

She parted the ribbons, allowing him a glimpse at her dusky, slick folds and the tight bud above her opening. He leaned closer, pumping his length in the same rhythm as she let her fingers dance on herself.

It looked beautiful. And it felt simply glorious.

He'd never seen Maya like this before, though he had seen her plenty of times with her legs open. She would never be like any other patient to him ever again. But at that moment, he couldn't care less. All he wanted was to thrust his throbbing cock into her hot, dripping hole in search of a release from this burning, torturous need that consumed him.

"Oh, God, I'm so close..." she moaned, sliding two fingers inside her, then rubbing faster, more fervently.

He pumped harder, too, imagining it was his cock not her fingers plunged inside her, coated slick with her arousal. He could almost taste her on his tongue. Oh, how he wished to taste her.

"Ahhh..." Air gushed out of her chest. Her mouth slackened. Her thighs trembled.

His desire spiked, his muscles tightening. He tossed his head so far back, it hit the high back of the couch. His horns stabbed through the leather.

A swell of bliss washed over him, sweeping all his senses. His growls blended with Maya's whimpers of joy.

Intense. Mind-blowing. Beautiful...

Her soft giggle came from the screen next—a caress to his ears. More than anything in the world right now, he wished to hold her.

She found her words first. "If you made it this far with me, if you watched the video to this point, you deserve to know. Your letters are making me fall in love with you all over again, Walter. So much deeper than ever before."

Walter?

The name slammed into him like a punch to his gut. He yanked his horns out of the couch and sat up straight.

The video actually wasn't meant for him?

The screen went blank. As Maya had warned at the beginning, the video disappeared after just one playback.

But hadn't *his* name been there, in the title of the video? Or did he dream seeing it? It wouldn't be much of a stretch—the entire video felt like a hot, sweaty, wonderful dream.

There was absolutely no reason for Maya to make it for him. It was far more logical to assume that she made it for her boyfriend back home. If so, Kear stole its one and only viewing. Now, it was burned into his brain.

Now, it was his and only his.

If only the woman in the video was his, too.

He couldn't tell when exactly it happened. But he wanted Maya more than he ever wanted anything or anyone in his life.

It would make so much sense if they were together. By a pure stroke of luck, she was even carrying his baby in her belly already.

Not many people knew that the most important fetus on Neron was biologically his. The parents of the fetus were listed only as male and female donors in all documentation. It aligned with both the protocol and his own preferences.

The embryo was a result of a long night working late with a string of failed tests.

He had tweaked the procedure and needed to know if his tweaks worked. But he'd run out of usable specimens of male sperm at the lab. He ended up using what he had on hand—his own sperm.

He'd just needed one more string of data to complete the sequence. After so many failures, he hadn't thought it would go very far. But it did. It had gone all the way to the nearly eight-month-long pregnancy that had every chance to result in a healthy baby very soon. *His* baby.

He'd never dreamed of being a father. Even now, he still couldn't believe it would happen. But he did what every Voranian father would do in his situation. He secured a spot for his child in the academy, booked aptitude tests, preordered an entire store's worth of baby stuff, and seeded the room closest to his bedroom with nursery-friendly plants.

All was ready for the baby to arrive, even if he still didn't feel entirely ready to become a father yet.

Chapter 18

Maya

For the first time in a very long time, there was no reply from Walter that morning. I kept checking my account over and over again while getting ready for my daily medical exam with Professor Thormus, but no messages popped up.

It couldn't be because of the video I'd sent. They said video files took a while to travel to Earth. Walter couldn't have received it yet. Something else must've happened.

On the other hand, until the past three months or so, it hadn't been unusual for me to go for weeks without hearing anything from Walter. There might be no need to worry yet.

I put on a hospital gown under my new fluffy robe, shoved my feet into my cozy slippers and waddled over to the elevators, then down a few floors to the lab with the exam room.

Daily examinations would be a huge overkill during a regular human pregnancy. But since this wasn't a regular pregnancy or even really a human one, Professor Thormus insisted on keeping a very close eye on it.

Being in my last month added pressure, too. We were nearing the finish line. Any negative incident could be so much more heartbreaking now.

"Hi Maya," Jazir, one of the technicians on Professor Thormus's team, greeted me as I entered the room.

"Morning."

Another technician waved in greeting as the third one adjusted the table height for me to climb on.

The professor's entire team consisted of men only. That was largely due to the demographics and lifestyle in Voran—women were few, and many of them chose not to work. The professor's personality might have something to do with it, as well. He seemed uncomfortable and awkward in female company unless they were his patients, which wouldn't entice his female colleagues into working with him.

"How are you today?" Jazir asked, helping me to lie down.

"Oh, you know, the usual." I shrugged. "I just keep *roly-polying* around as best as I can."

Jazir laughed, then the stomping of the professor's hooves announced his arrival.

"Morning," he barked out, not really addressing anyone.

He seemed to try especially hard to avoid my eyes as he pushed some buttons on the machines around the examination table, swiped through some charts on the screens, then snapped some gloves on.

"How are you today, Professor?" I asked as he stepped to the foot of the table, taking his usual position in front of my bent legs.

He nodded, without even a glance at my face. I wished I could do the same, just ignore him and let him do his job. Instead, I was taking in his tall figure, admiring how tightly his lab coverall hugged his wide shoulders and how beautifully the harsh lighting in the room reflected in his eyes.

"Well..." He jerked his head, as if his neckline was too tight for his neck, then placed a hand on my knee.

Breath left me in a gush. Heat rushed down my body.

I had tried so hard not to think about him when touching myself last night. But every time I'd conjured Walter's face in my mind, it would immediately grow horns, its human features quickly turning into the professor's scowl. The moment that happened, my lust had shot into the highest gear, delivering the best orgasm I'd ever had.

It was all I could do not to say "Kear" again instead of "Walter" at the end of the video.

The purpose of me making that video in the first place had been to redirect my sexual fantasy to the man they should be about. But it backfired badly. Kear had been the one I dreamed about last night. And he was all I could think about right now.

My awareness rushed to the spot where the professor's hand rested on my bare knee. Heat from his touch seeped to my skin through his glove.

He tapped the inside of my knee with his thumb, twice. "Open for me, Maya."

I gasped at the rasp in his voice. A rush of tingling pleasure swirled low in my belly. He shot his gaze to my face, finally, as if catching himself feeling the same.

It wasn't right for either of us to feel anything at all in this situation.

Only why did it feel so right to stare into his eyes, then?

He looked like he knew and understood everything.

He also looked like he was about to drop the probe he was holding and bolt out of the room.

"Professor?"

Kear

THERE SHE WAS, SPREAD out for him...to examine. Not to ogle. Not to fantasize about last night's video. And definitely not to touch the way he wished to touch her.

Her gaze moved to his hand on her knee where he found his thumb tracing circles over her skin.

"Professor?" she asked again, tentatively.

Was he scaring her now? Staring at her like a mindless dummy?

His mind certainly seemed to have deserted him.

Focus, Kear.

He dragged his eyes away from her face, over the mound of her belly, then down to her core.

She wasn't wearing any panties; she never did for the exam. Only it didn't feel like any other of the hundreds of examinations he'd performed on her before.

It felt like he saw her, really saw all of her, for the first time ever. His nostrils flared and his mouth watered. He wished he could bury his face between her thighs to revel in her scent and taste.

"Is anything wrong, Professor?" Jazir asked quietly for only him to hear.

Maya looked alarmed. Her dark eyes were open wide, her pupils dilated. Her chest heaved with shallow breaths. She bit on her bottom lip, staring at him intently.

Only was it really alarm she was feeling?

The look of her brought back the images from the video to his mind. She looked flushed. Tense... Just like she did last night.

Was she *aroused?*

He groaned inwardly. How was he supposed to do his job now?

Focus, Kear.

He gripped her knee, getting a better hold on the probe in his other hand. Then forced his eyes down to her slick, warm, glistening puss—

No. He couldn't fucking allow himself to think that way.

He drew in a long breath, shaking his head, then looked down again at his subject's *reproductive organ.*

He was a fucking professional. A renowned scientist. A doctor who'd treated hundreds of women in his career. He'd seen enough female *genitals* to calm the fuck down and not turn into a horny sweating kid at the sight of one.

"Everything is fine." He swallowed hard and slipped the probe into Maya's wet, tight, enticing hole...um, *birth canal.*

The short fur on his forehead slicked with sweat. His breathing was shallow, just like hers.

"It's fine," he repeated, even as no one asked him again. "I'm fine. Everything is fine." He blinked, slightly angling the probe inside her.

She released a soft whimper, adjusting her hips. He snapped his eyes to hers, finding hers hooded and dark.

This wasn't simply an exam for her, either.

The idea that Maya might be just as affected by him as he was by her made him feel light-headed.

What if she did make that video for *him*, after all?

His hand trembled, and he jerked the probe out of her, even as the machines had no time to collect the data on the current condition of the internal environment for the fetus to thrive. He'd have to calculate the necessary adjustments to her daily supplement requirement later.

The exam wasn't done yet, but he was. He had to leave the room immediately lest he bury his face between her legs and stretch his tongue down her tempting *birth canal* all the way to tickle her cervix.

Fuck...

He had to get out.

The last thing he needed was for his team to witness his loss of self-control and for the word to spread that the world-renowned Professor Thormus was in fact a slimeball pervert who lusted after his patients.

He had a stellar reputation. Never in his entire career had he allowed himself so much as an improper thought toward any men or women he'd treated. And now, an entire barrage of nasty, dirty, outright filthy thoughts about things he'd love to do to this alluring human woman threatened to bury him alive.

"Finish without me," he barked at Jazir, tossing the used probe onto a tray.

Spinning on his hoof, he stomped to the door.

"Professor, wait!" Maya scrambled from the table. "Please."

She hurried out into the corridor after him.

"I'm so sorry," the words rushed out of her. "That was highly inappropriate of me. I promise it will never happen again. I didn't mean..."

What the fuck was *she* apologizing for?

She grabbed his sleeve, leaving him no choice but to stop and face her if he didn't want to drag her along the corridor with him.

Her face flushed, she gazed at him with those dark eyes of hers. His heart ached, swelling with tenderness at her pained expression.

"You did nothing wrong, my fl—" He stopped himself, barely in time. "Maya."

Her eyes bounced from him to the wall on his left, then on his right.

"I didn't mean to moan. With your probe inside my...um...me. My body." She wrung her hands in front of her.

A growl vibrated deep in his throat. His coverall grew dangerously tight around his hips, his cock demanding more space in the crotch.

She was regretting it. Even if she was affected by him, she didn't want to be.

He scraped a hand down his face. "It wasn't your fault."

Maybe if he didn't fantasize about fucking her during the exam, he wouldn't have practically caressed her with that probe in the first place.

Her cheeks turned ruddy and probably dangerously hot.

"It must be the pregnancy hormones," she muttered apologetically.

How could a woman look even more beautiful when she was flustered like that? He wished to gather her in his arms and kiss that shy expression off her face, then make her moan and whimper some more.

"Must be." He rubbed his right horn, tearing his eyes away from her lips.

"I promise it will never happen again."

"Why not?" he blurted out.

Her eyes flared with shock.

"What are you talking about, Professor?"

"I mean... I don't mind you moaning from my touch. In fact, I wish to hear more of it." What the fuck was he saying? It came out weird.

Creepy? Definitely clumsy. "In private, of course. Without my team around," he added, possibly making it even worse.

She stared at him wide-eyed.

"Professor...I..."

"*Kear*, Maya. Please call me Kear."

"Kear?" she sounded as if tasting his name on her tongue, and he loved it coming from her mouth.

"Yes," he said softly. "Like friends do. We are friends, aren't we?"

She had certainly become his best friend by now. But there was so much more he wished she could be.

"Friends," she echoed, glancing aside. "*Friends* is good. Let's stick to that."

No, this was bad. And he'd walked right into it.

"Maya, no—"

She shook her head so fast, he feared she might twist her neck.

"Friends are all we could be, Kear. I'm in love with Walter. We're well on the way to mending our relationship. I don't want to jeopardize that."

"Actually, about that..." He squeezed the back of his neck so hard, his fingers dug deep into the muscle.

By taking over her correspondence with her ex, he'd given her hope. It had helped her thrive, overcoming the heartache. But he'd also ruined any chance he could ever have with her. Because when she finally learned the truth, she'd hate his guts. Rightfully so.

She heaved a sigh. "I'll be completely honest with you, Kear. I do have feelings for you. But this, whatever it is..." She waved a hand between them, her words slicing through him like a surgical laser. "It's just a temporary physical attraction that surely would lead nowhere. Trust me, it's not worth losing our friendship over. I didn't come to Neron for some quick romp in the sack with a hot alien. And you deserve so much better than that—"

The sound of a door opening cut her off. Jazir poked his head out from the exam room.

"Professor? Maya? Are we completing today's examination?" his assistant asked.

"Yes," Kear replied firmly.

No matter what, he had to go on with his work, even without a fully functioning heart in his chest now.

"Um..." Maya hesitated, then delivered another blow both to his heart and his ego. "I think it'd be best if Jazir completed the exam instead of you."

His hackles rose at the idea of another man touching her, even if in a strictly medical way.

"Actually," she continued, clearly intending to end him today. "I think it would be best if Jazir or someone else from the team did all my exams from now on."

Chapter 19

Maya

"*Dear Maya,*

I'm afraid I won't be able to write to you for a while. I don't wish to stop our correspondence. Writing to you has become a necessity for me. I need to have this connection with you more than I need air. But I must step back and find the strength to speak with you in person before I write another word to you.

Whatever happens, please know you have become a huge part of my life. You've warmed my heart and brightened my existence. Nothing and no one would ever change that.

You are and will always be my beautiful flower. The most beautiful in the whole of the Universe."

I had no idea what to make of this. It didn't sound at all like his last break-up letter. Yet the hint of sadness in his words felt like he might be saying goodbye.

I re-read the letter at least a dozen times. His sweet words left no doubt he cared about me and appreciated what we had. He wished to talk to me in person. Maybe we could do a video call from the spaceship on my way back to Earth?

It wasn't long now until I'd be heading back home, with my pregnancy being in its ninth month already.

The letter stayed on my mind, but not as much as it would have had it not been for Kear. The professor proved to be a very persistent distraction, no matter how hard I tried to get him out of my head.

After our last conversation in the hallway in front of the exam room, he gave me space, just like I'd asked. He remained present in the room during all my morning exams that followed, but kept his distance, letting Jazir handle any equipment that came into physical contact with my body.

Kear still met me for lunch daily as it had become a tradition between us. But he no longer ate with me. He'd just have a quick cup of tea, catching up on his usual questions about my wellbeing, then retreat back to his lab. Needless to say, there hadn't been any outings to the city for us in the past few days, either.

I understood it was what we needed to do. But I missed our conversations and spending time together.

Not being an exceptionally outgoing person, it always took me a long time to build a connection with anyone. Kear wasn't quick to make friends, either. Despite all of that, we had found so many things that drew us together. And now, we had to let it all go, which proved excruciatingly painful.

Just as I had feared, the physical attraction had ruined our platonic friendship, and now I missed it.

I missed him.

The whole ordeal had dampened my excitement in anticipation of the assembly gala. When the day had finally come, however, I was glad to be going out again.

Stopping at Kear's door, I adjusted my evening gown over my enormous belly and knocked. His AI screen lit up on the wall.

"Hi, buddy." I waved at it. "It's me, Maya."

The door opened, and Kear was standing behind it. Dressed in a smart black suit with dark-purple swirls, he looked more handsome than ever. Unable to help myself, I swept my gaze up from his polished hooves, to the shiny buttons of his suit coat, the crisp white shirt peeking out above the collar, and to the blue-and-silver stars painted on his horns.

"Wow…" I exhaled. "You clean up nicely, Professor."

"Thanks." He cleared his throat, shifting on his hooves uneasily, obviously unused to responding to compliments on his appearance.

I smoothed my hands down my green-apple gown decorated with pink and purple flowers along the off-shoulder neckline. The same flowers were scattered along the hemline. A golden cord served as a belt right under my breasts since with my ever-expanding middle, that was now the thinnest part of my torso.

The summer colors of my outfit made me feel happy. But I feared that next to the tall and elegant Kear, I might look like a round flower bed.

"Let's hope a bird doesn't mistake me for a bush and try to make a nest on my head." I quipped.

Kear's violet eyes opened wide, drawing me in.

"Maya, you are the most beautiful woman I've ever seen." He said it so earnestly, it was impossible not to believe him.

Still I asked, "Even in this state?" I gestured with both hands down at my belly.

"In *any* state," he replied with unwavering confidence. "You really have no idea how beautiful you are. And it's not just the looks... Frankly, I have no idea either what exactly makes you so beautiful to me. But you take my breath away when I look at you. You remind me of a flower that may need some time to open up but is the most amazing to behold once it happens."

His words echoed through my mind as something I'd heard before, though I couldn't remember where. His eyes trapped me, making it hard to focus.

I smiled, glancing aside.

He tapped my chin with his finger. "This smile is too tiny. It doesn't show your dimples."

"My dimples?" Didn't Walter say something about that in one of his letters? This whole conversation was now giving me a strong feeling of déjà vu.

"Well, shall we?" Kear took me under my arm, leading me toward the landing platform with his aircraft. "Let's make the most of this evening. I hope to hear your laugh tonight, for those dimples to show up."

THE VENUE OF THE ASSEMBLY was a huge terrace on top of a tall building of an academic institution.

Kear parked his aircraft by attaching it to the edge of the terrace, then helped me off it. He led me along a large open space already set with tables and chairs for the dinner after the formal part with speeches.

We descended a set of wide stairs toward the sunken stage surrounded by cascading rows of seating in the style of an amphitheater. People mingled around, some sitting down, others standing and strolling in between. The dark evening sky glistened through the glass dome above us. The moment we appeared, conversations stopped and all attention turned to us.

The stage remained empty for now.

"Is that where you're going to do your presentation?" I asked Kear quietly.

He nodded but had no chance to reply. A man rushed to us from an upper row.

"Madam Maya Gupta!"

"Egus," Kear grumped under his breath.

Professor Egus beamed, grabbing my hand in both of his.

"It's so, so nice to see you again. I can't believe Thormus actually let you out of the dungeon in his clinic."

Kear scoffed. "There is no dungeon in my clinic."

"Well," I gave both a pacifying smile. "It did feel rather restrictive at the hospital in the beginning. But I did get out quite a bit after that.

The main reason I stay in nowadays is this one." I gently petted my belly.

As if sensing my touch, the baby kicked, and I gasped softly.

"Are you alright?" Kear gripped my elbow, his thick eyebrows immediately moving into a frown of concern.

"Oh, it's fine." I laughed. "We just woke up my little tenant, that's all."

"The fetus is moving, then?" Professor Egus's eyes followed my hand with an undisguised curiosity. "Is it active?"

"Very active. Lately especially—" I cut myself short, realizing that Kear remained quiet on the baby's condition.

Maybe there were some concerns he didn't want to talk about? Or maybe he didn't want to share the details with Egus? Either way, I decided it was best to keep my mouth shut, too.

"Are you giving a speech, too, tonight, Professor Egus?" I asked instead.

"Me? No." He shook his head with a somewhat exaggerated laugh. "Ever since you came along, dear Madam Maya, no one cares about what I have to say. This assembly only has eyes and ears for Thormus now. As does the press."

There was a bitter note in his voice, despite the friendly smile lingering on his face.

"We should sit down," Kear said, pointing at the two seats in the first row.

"You can sit with me, Madam Maya," Egus offered.

"She has a perfectly good seat right here," Kear barked, slapping a hand on the seat next to his.

"But she'll end up sitting alone when you go on stage."

"She'll come with me."

I tilted my head at him. "I will?"

That was news to me.

"Of course you will." He met my eyes. "All these people will tear me apart if I don't present you to them. Just look at the crowd." He swept with his gaze along the rows around the stage. Every single face of those present was turned to us. "Trust me, I wouldn't get this much attention if I were here without you."

"Well." Professor Egus bowed his head to me. "We'll catch up after dinner then, Maya. Maybe luck will smile upon me tonight and you'll agree to dance with me."

"The best I can offer is some swaying and shuffling, in my condition." I grinned, gesturing at my belly. "If you don't mind that, I'll be happy to dance with you."

He flashed me a smile while Kear growled like a dog with a bone.

"You dislike Egus, don't you?" I lowered my voice as we took our seats. "Why? Did he do something to you in the past?"

He shrugged, then admitted reluctantly. "No. Nothing to hold a grudge over. It's just a feeling. I don't trust him."

"Sounds like an unexplained animosity. Due to your grumpy nature, maybe? If so, you should simply remember your manners and behave. Egus seems nice."

He scowled. "Too nice." But then conceded, "He's alright, I guess. Better than that scoundrel Hezer."

I had no time to ask who Hezer was and what made him a "scoundrel" because a voice announced, "Let's welcome our Governor Ashir Kaeya Drustan with Madam Governor."

As per Voranian custom, a married woman not only took her husband's name but also attached his title to her honorifics. Like I'd be Madam Professor Thormus if I married Kear—

What a random thought that was. Completely uncalled for and out of place. I shook my head, hoping to rid my brain of any notion like that.

A couple entered. The man was all smiles. He waved at the crowd and winked at Kear as if they were buddies. Which, judging by Kear's reaction, they were not. Respectful but distant, the professor grunted uneasily and bowed his head.

Madam Governor was a tall woman, who appeared to be in the middle of her own pregnancy. A burgundy dress with gold embroidery flowed over the slight swell of her belly. She smiled at Kear and me, taking a seat next to her husband across the stage from us.

"Is she one of your patients?" I asked Kear.

"No. Not this pregnancy of hers. I had to decline looking after her this time."

"Why?"

"I had no time for another patient," he replied simply. "And there is no reason to expect any complications with her pregnancy. It progresses well. Another doctor is taking care of her. She doesn't need me."

I knew he was incredibly busy. Looking after me had taken most of his working time, leaving hardly anything left for his regular patients. Yet I also knew that he had other patients, like the sister of that man we'd ran into in the shopping mall. That woman was a far less glamorous patient than the wife of the country's governor, but she really needed his skills and expertise, so he'd taken her on, despite being busy.

Kear obviously didn't put status as a priority when selecting his patients. Instead, he took those who needed him most.

"Professor Kear Umhra Thormus," the organizer announced.

Kear took my hand, rising to his hooves.

"Do you really want me to come with you?" I whispered, feeling suddenly apprehensive as the public attention seemed to intensify tenfold. "It's you they want to hear."

"Everything I'm planning to say is about you. If it weren't for you, none of it would happen."

I climbed to my feet. As if to prove his words, the space immediately erupted into cheers and applause. The Voranians stomped their hooves in approval, creating such a racket, I wondered how the floor didn't collapse.

"See?" Kear smiled.

As much as he disliked people's attention, he seemed to genuinely enjoy their appreciation of me.

I smiled, awkwardly bowing my head to the crowd as he led me to the center of the stage.

"Madam Maya Gupta," he introduced me loudly.

The cheers intensified. With a nervous giggle, I bowed once again. Despite what Kear had said, I didn't feel deserving of all this enthusiasm. I couldn't really take credit for my uterus being so cooperative with Kear's efforts. But I just smiled and waved, accepting their gratitude.

A drone descended toward the stage from the upper rows. A holographic screen fanned out above it, displaying a complicated chart with a gazillion labels in Voranian language.

"The current state of our study," Kear announced. With a few hand gestures he made some parts of the chart bigger, explaining the numbers and highlighting the difference between a normal Voranian pregnancy and mine.

He kept it short, probably mindful of me standing next to him. The moment he finished, several hands rose in the air. The assembly drone registered them, putting them into a queue for questions.

The charts were gone from the screen, and a list of names appeared instead. The first person, a woman with an armband I'd seen reporters wear on TV, rose from her seat.

"Madam Maya Gupta, what do you think about the study?"

"Me?" I glanced at Kear, and he gave me an encouraging nod. "Well, I'm happy to be here. I mean, I'm glad I'm able to help."

A man jumped before the woman even managed to react to my answer. "What compelled you to participate in it? Money?"

Kear growled softly. But I wasn't taken aback by the man's assertive tone.

"Money certainly didn't hurt," I said. "Initially, it might've been my main motivation. But the more I get to know your country and your people, the more excited I am about doing something positive for the Voranians and their human spouses. It's a good thing. And I'm happy to be a part of it."

Another man got up when his name came up on the list. "As someone outside of the Voranian culture, will you find it difficult to part from the baby after giving birth to it?"

"I came here as a surrogate, not a future mother. That's the state of mind I've been in ever since. Of course, it's impossible not to get attached to some degree." I placed a hand on my belly, smoothing the ache from another kick of a tiny hoof inside. "But I'm looking forward to delivering a happy, healthy baby for an expecting couple."

"Do you know who the parents of the baby are?"

"No, I don't…" I looked at Kear again, but he volunteered no information on that. "It depends on their contract with the study team, I suppose."

Kear lifted his hand. "No more questions. Maya has stood here long enough. She needs a break to rest."

Standing for a prolonged period of time was tiring, but being in the spotlight of everyone's attention was worse. It got really overwhelming after a while.

We hadn't made it even a quarter down the list of the people who wished to ask questions. In a rising panic, people jumped from their seats, shouting their questions at us.

"Maya, how much longer are you planning to stay on Neron after the baby's birth?"

I shook my head. "I haven't decided yet."

"Will you accept Professor Thormus's invitation to stay for another month?"

"She said she hasn't decided," Kear barked, gripping my elbow. "No more questions." Holding an arm in front of him like a shield, he maneuvered me through the crowd that was now taking over the stage. "You did great," he said softly into my ear on the way to our seats. "I'm so proud of you, my flower."

The nickname tugged with warmth and longing at my heart, the way it did when I saw it in Walter's letters. I loved the new nickname that he'd given me. It wasn't a common one, and it was only between Walter and me.

Why would Kear suddenly start calling me that, too?

The noise of the crowd, the lights in my face, and his insistent tugging at my arm as Kear tried to get me into my seat—all of it finally became too much. Doubts buzzed in my mind like a swarm of bees.

"I need to get out of here," I whispered to Kear.

"Are you not feeling well?"

"It's the noise. It's just too much."

"This way." He stirred me to the left, then opened the door on the side of the stairs. Turning to the crowd following us, he raised his hand. "Give her some space," he growled. "There will be some time for your questions later."

The crowd ebbed, and he ushered me through the door out into the level below the patio, behind the seating.

It was dark here. The only light came from outside. The night cityscape filled the huge windows that surrounded a circular space behind the seats of the arena with the stage. This floor must serve as an observation deck, but also as storage because the spare folding tables were neatly stacked along a wall.

"Any pain?" Kear asked in a clipped voice of a doctor. "Dizziness? Cramps?"

"No." I looked into his eyes. They were dark purple here in the semi-darkness but as beautiful as ever.

"Something is bothering you," he stated.

How could I describe this weird feeling nagging at the back of my brain? I couldn't put a finger on it, and that was the most irritating.

"Maya, what's wrong? Are you restless? Tired? Do you want to leave? It's late. You need your rest."

You need your rest...

You have to take care of yourself...

Not the exact words, but the tone was the same—caring. And my response to them was similar. They made me feel warm and safe. Cherished. The way Kear spoke evoked the same feelings I had when reading Walter's letters.

And that nickname... *Flower.*

It couldn't possibly be a coincidence.

I never assumed my correspondence with Walter was absolutely private. They'd warned me that all interplanetary messages were scanned for security purposes. It didn't worry me, since I didn't include any discussions on political or military topics or whatever else would be considered unacceptable by the Liaison Committee. I never considered, however, that as the head of the study, Kear might have access to my communication with my boyfriend.

"You've read my letters to Walter." I held his gaze, searching those pretty eyes for any sign of denial.

He winced, halting his breath.

I shook my head. "Just tell me the truth, Kear. Please. Did you read Walter's letters?"

"No," he said and added before I could feel any sense of relief, "I *wrote* them."

Chapter 20

Maya

"You what?" I choked on the question. Kear wrote Walter's letters?

That wasn't the truth I had expected. It made no sense.

"I didn't just read those letters, Maya. For the past three and a half months, I wrote them all."

Stunned, I could only utter, "Why?"

He raked his hands through the fur on his head, skimming around his star-sparkling horns.

"I found you crying over one of *his* letters—"

"So, you thought you could write better?" My voice rose with disbelief.

"But I *did* write better. Look at you. You're smiling, laughing, thriving. You're happy."

"Happy to be lied to?"

The world was spinning in a slow circle. The night air seemed to thicken, like a dark whirlpool dragging me under.

The door to the auditorium opened and Jazir poked his head in.

"Professor, Governor Drustan would like to speak with you."

Kear stabbed his fingers through his fur again, then gripped his horns with a growl. "Fuck the Governor."

Jazir froze, blinking in astonishment.

"Go, Kear," I said, biting my lip. "It sounds important."

"Nothing is more important than *this*." He gestured between us.

I struggled to breathe.

I thought I was falling in love with the man behind those letters. But it was all a lie. There was no man to fall in love with. Kear made him up.

Walter never heard from me and never responded. For all I knew, he'd been living a happy single life for months now or worse, dating someone else already.

"How long have you been doing this, you said? Three and a half months? Is that how long you've been making a fool out of me?"

He winced as if I'd slapped him.

"Maya. Please don't think about it like that."

"Don't you tell me what to *think*! Isn't it enough that you've manipulated what I've been *feeling*?" Maybe I *should* slap him? He certainly deserved it. "You had no business writing those letters or reading mine. I didn't write them for you." A sudden thought pierced through my chest with alarm and mortification. "And the video? Oh, my God, please don't tell me you watched the video, too."

At my mention of the video, his eyelids hooded his gaze. His tongue slipped out, licking his lips. And I knew for a fact that he'd watched it.

Tingles of arousal skittered down my bare arms, poking holes in the shroud of my embarrassment. I diverted some of my anger at him toward myself. How could I still be turned on by this guy, even after everything that had just come to light?

"The video had *my* name on it," he stated with emphasis.

"What?" I felt sick to my stomach. "No, it didn't! Why the hell would I put your name on it? It wasn't meant for you!"

"I don't know why. But you did. It said *'For Kear's eyes only.'*"

The point of that video was to get my mind off him. I had tried so hard *not* to think about him when I made it.

Had I failed so completely? Had I subconsciously addressed my private video to the professor instead of my boyfriend?

It seemed highly possible, which made everything so much worse. I groaned, shaking with anger and burning with mortification.

Someone cleared their throat by the door. "Um..."

I realized Jazir was still there, holding the door ajar.

"I beg your pardon, Professor. I know this isn't a good time, but Governor—"

Kear roared, really roared like a feral beast, stomping his hoof and angling his horns at poor Jazir, who now held the door like a shield between them.

"Kear, you should go." I gestured at the door. He jerked his head to me, but I wouldn't let him say a word. "Go. Get out of here. I honestly can't see your face right now."

His shoulders sagged, like the air had deflated from him, taking his irritation too. His voice softened.

"I'm not leaving you alone."

I strained to keep it together. "Trust me, that is the best you can do for me right now. Get the fuck out of here!"

Jazir froze, his eyes open wide in shock. He'd never seen me so angry before. I didn't remember ever feeling this enraged, either.

Kear seemed to be taken aback, too. He nodded, retreating to the door.

"Take a few minutes. Focus on your breathing—"

"Fuck off, Kear," I snapped.

Turning my back to him, I walked over to one of the huge windows and pressed my forehead to the cool glass. Closing my eyes, I tried not to think about any of it. My blood boiled with anger at Kear, yet I did what he'd said, breathing slowly in and out.

The door behind me opened again.

"I said go away," I mumbled without turning around.

"I will if you insist," Professor Egus, not Kear, spoke behind me. "But I think you may need company."

"Why would you think so?" I made an effort to pull myself together before turning to face him.

He smiled, somewhat sheepishly. "I happened to be close to the door when Jazir held it open. Forgive me, but I overheard Thormus raising his voice at you."

He did raise his voice. But I yelled, too. It was a nasty argument, one that wasn't even over yet.

I scraped a hand down my face. Oh, what a mess this was.

Professor Egus came closer.

"I'm sorry he upset you, though I'm not surprised that he did. In fact, I was expecting something like that to happen much sooner."

"Why?"

"Many of us in the scientific community lack social skills to some degree. It comes from the nature of our occupation—we tend to live in our heads more than in the real world. But with Thormus, it's especially obvious. With colleagues, he manages to interact with some efficiency. But I had little faith in his abilities when he attempted to build a friendship with you outside of his study."

My heart pinched with sadness. I glanced back at the window to hide my expression. I'd cherished my friendship with Kear. But it had fallen apart already, even before I'd discovered how he'd walked all over my trust and my feelings, stomped all over them with those polished hooves of his.

"Whatever he did," Professor Egus continued, "you didn't deserve it. I'm very sorry he spoiled what was supposed to be a lovely evening. May I offer myself as your dinner date after all? I promise to do my best to salvage the situation and ensure you have fun while dancing tonight."

"It's very kind of you, Professor Egus, but I'm afraid I'm no longer in a dancing mood. I'll be leaving as soon as possible."

Dinner and dance might help to put Kear and his lies out of my head for a while. But all I really wished to do right now was to lock myself in my apartment and eat unhealthy amounts of healthy hospital food. Sadly, there was no hope of getting any cupcakes at this time of the night.

"In this case, allow me to fly you home," Professor Egus offered.

Would his company be any better than Kear's? Kear had a strong possessive streak when it came to me, at least for the duration of the study. He'd hate for me to leave with the man he largely disliked for no apparent reason.

The idea of pissing Kear off brought some satisfaction, but it flitted away quickly. Deep inside, I knew that hurting him in retaliation wouldn't really make me feel any better in the long run.

"Thank you, but I'll wait for Ke...for Professor Thormus to fly me back to the hospital."

"He'll probably stay for the rest of the evening. He needs to mingle with all the important people now, since he's been pretty much the star of every assembly since you came along. Me, on the other hand..." He smiled. "I'm free to leave anytime I please. No one would miss me."

Still, it didn't feel right leaving with Egus. I barely knew him.

He noticed my hesitation. "At the very least, please let me call you a taxi."

That seemed like the optimal solution. Taking a taxi aircraft meant I wouldn't have to endure Kear's company on the way back to the hospital. The less I saw of that man tonight, the better.

I nodded. "Thank you. That would work."

Egus stepped aside to the nearest AI drone and placed an order for a taxi out of my earshot while I stared out the window again.

It was hard to process the elaborate lie that had stretched over the past three and a half months. How could I have been so wrong about Kear? I thought I knew him. I thought he cared about me, at least a little bit. But all he really cared about was his work and what I represented in it.

"All set." Professor Egus headed back to me.

I sniffled and quickly wiped off an errant tear from my cheek.

"Great. Thank you."

He cupped my elbow. "Allow me to escort you to the aircraft."

Thankfully, we didn't have to return to the stage area. The last thing I wanted was to face the crowd with my eyes swollen and my nose running.

Instead, Professor Egus took me up a narrow staircase on the side of the room. We exited onto the rooftop terrace with the tables ready for a lavish dinner. My stomach spasmed at the thought of eating dinner while sitting next to Kear and thinking about what he'd done.

I absolutely had to leave.

"This way, please." Egus led me to an aircraft parked at the edge of the terrace.

As was typical for the Voranian taxies operated by an AI, the aircraft had no driver. I climbed into the passenger's seat and found the seat belt.

"Would you let Professor Thormus know I left, please?" I asked Egus.

Unexpectedly, he climbed into the driver's seat.

"I'm coming with you," he announced, promptly bringing the aircraft into motion.

"What? Why?" I bristled.

It wasn't what we'd agreed on.

"It's best that I personally escort you, Maya."

"I'd be just fine on my own," I snapped, annoyed at him for forcing his company on me when all I wanted tonight was to be left alone.

"Probably," he retorted. "But isn't being with me more fun than sulking all alone?"

Irritation buzzed through me. I found Egus pleasant enough. And normally, I wouldn't have minded his company. But I didn't appreciate how pushy he acted right now.

Turning away from him, I stared into the night illuminated by the city lights. There was nothing I could say that wouldn't potentially start an argument, so I kept quiet.

Heartbroken from Kear's deception and irritated by Egus's behavior, I didn't pay much attention to where we were traveling. After a while, it felt like the sprawling building of the hospital should have come into view already. But it was nowhere in sight.

"Where are we going?" I asked Egus.

"Just a small detour." He flashed me a smile. "I hope you don't mind."

"Oh, I do mind," I protested. "I want to go back to my apartment." I didn't leave a busy dinner party to go on a night tour with a man who was largely still a stranger. "I'm tired and want to be alone."

"And I will deliver you right back to that dreadful hospital as promised. After a short stop on the way."

"A short stop where?"

We had flown all the way to the edge of the city, it seemed. The buildings here were shorter and spread wider, with a complete darkness lying beyond.

"Right there." Egus pointed at the tall tower that stuck out from the sea of low-rise buildings.

"What's there?"

"Just one of the many places where I do my work. It'd be an honor to welcome you to my lab."

Apprehension tensed my muscles.

"Your bringing me here like this is not 'welcoming,' Professor. What you're doing is kidnapping."

"Oh." He looked genuinely offended. "That's such a harsh word, Madam Maya Gupta."

"It's not just a word. Kidnapping is a crime. I don't consent to you bringing me here. Take me back to the hospital right now."

He pouted but didn't whir off course, steering the aircraft straight toward the rooftop of the tower.

"It won't take long."

Dread prickled my skin with icy needles.

"*What* won't take long? What are you planning to do with me?"

Chapter 21

Maya

Egus all but dragged me out of the aircraft and under the glass dome over the rooftop of the high tower on the other side of Voran City. It was far away from the hospital and the assembly building where he'd taken me from.

"You won't get away with this," I seethed. "Kear will be furious when he finds out."

"*If* he finds out," a voice came from the door behind a tall lattice draped with dry vines, then the owner of the voice appeared. The man was shorter than Egus and more stout, but he held himself with much more self-assurance than my kidnapper. "Which I'll make sure never happens. *Kear*, as you call him, will never know what happened to you."

Said softly, his words didn't sound like a threat, more like a statement of fact, which made them only more terrifying, as if this man held my life in his hands, and he had already decided it wouldn't end well.

Dread spiked into fear inside me.

"Who are you?"

He smirked, then gave me a formal bow before introducing himself.

"Professor Hezer, a far more renowned and distinguished scholar in my field than your *Kear* can ever hope to be."

I cocked a hip, folding my arms over my chest. "Yet *he's* the one being honored at the assembly right now. While you're here, kidnapping his study subject."

His lips twitched, wiping the smirk off his face.

"It was nothing but damn luck on his part," he sneered. "I spent much more time working on this—"

"You didn't go to war, then? Was that how you got more time than Kear to work on your research? And still, you failed."

He jerked his head, his tail lashing around his hooves.

"I didn't fail! He got fucking lucky, literally stumbling upon the breakthrough before anyone else."

"Well, lucky or not, he's ahead now and there is nothing you can do about it."

"Unless he suffers a setback." His face split with a smile, and I did not like the look of it. "He hasn't delivered a live birth yet. I can still get ahead."

My insides seemed to turn to ice at his words.

"What are you talking about?"

Egus shifted his hooves uneasily.

"We'll just take a few tests, Maya."

I drew in a shaky breath. I couldn't allow them to touch me. I had to get out of here.

But how?

Jumping back into the aircraft would do little to help me escape. It was now clear that the aircraft belonged to Egus. It wasn't a taxi. I couldn't operate it, and even if I could get it airborne somehow, Egus might be able to change its course remotely. Or I might crash.

Doing my best to keep my panic under control, I slowly side-stepped Professor Hezer toward the door to the room he'd come out of. If I made it there, I could possibly use the AI to call for help. Every building in Voran was equipped with AI. They should have one here, too.

"What kind of tests?" I had to keep them distracted while progress-ing toward the door.

Hezer waved me off. "You wouldn't understand."

"Sure I wouldn't," I scoffed sarcastically, shifting just a little more to the left. "I only have been subjected to a million of tests in the past eight and a half months, or longer, if you count my five-month journey to this planet and all the preliminary tests I did while still on Earth. How could I possibly know anything about the procedure?" I threw my hands up in the air, dramatically, while gaining a few more inches around Hezer on my way to the door. "Kear... I mean Professor Thormus has measured anything and everything possible already. And he's just made his latest results public. What could you possibly still be missing?"

"Not all results have been made public, sweetie," Hezer muttered. "The fucking crook is holding some things back. But we will find out what it is."

He moved toward me, and I dashed for the door.

With my belly in the way, "dashing" wasn't nearly as fast as I wished it to be.

The space behind the door opened up into a huge room. Set with long narrow stands with screens and work areas and divided by shelf units with tubes and vials, it looked like a lab. It was similar to Kear's workroom in his apartment at the hospital, only about ten times bigger from what I could see.

I bumped into a stand, knocking it over. The screens shattered. A few vials of liquid spilled on the floor.

The stomping of hooves behind me halted.

"What are you doing?" Hezer yelled. "You wrecked it!"

"Good. Serves you right." I shoved against another stand. A screen device fell off, cracking on impact with the floor. A pyramid of glass tubes shook, clinking ominously.

"Don't break it!" Egus pleaded.

"You'll pay for it, wretched human," Hezer growled.

I kicked with my elbow against the glass pyramid, sending it off the stand.

"Stop it!" Hezer screeched as the glass exploded into shards, spraying the clear liquid over the green floor tiles.

"Oops," I mocked, shoving yet another stand their way.

Hezer cursed loudly while Egus scrambled to catch whatever he could from the stand before it keeled over. He looked ready to cry, but it failed to stir any sympathy in me. If he didn't want the destruction, he shouldn't have brought me here.

Shoving shelf units aside, I made my way through the lab, searching for the exit.

A drone whirred by me.

"Welcome, Professor Egus, Professor Hezer." It turned its milky-white screen toward me as I ran by. "Greetings, visitor."

"Call Professor Thormus," I yelled at it.

The name came to me automatically. I had no time to consider whom to call for help. But even if I had, Kear would be my best bet, considering the circumstances. They all were colleagues here. There was a good chance that Kear's name and contact information were stored in Egus's drone's database.

The connecting signal sounded, sending a jolt of hope through me.

"Yes?" Kear picked up immediately.

His voice sounded strained. Even that one word conveyed to me that he wasn't at the dinner party having fun. He was stressed.

"Kear!" I shouted.

"Cut the call," Hezer ordered, and the drone fell silent, my one connection with the outside world severed. "Get over here now, human, or it'll be worse."

I made sure to keep a few stands and shelves between us. "How much worse?"

"Maya, please, stop this destruction and cooperate," Egus intervened.

"Why would I?" I had not a crumb of faith in them caring about either the baby or me. Giving them any control over my body would be a huge mistake.

"Fuck it!" Hezer shoved a stand out of his way and leaped toward me.

More of their equipment dropped and shattered, but he didn't seem to care about that anymore. Getting me took priority over everything else for him.

I jumped out of his way, but Egus blocked my escape. I had no choice but to spin around and dash back to the rooftop.

The two exited after me. They were no longer running, confident that they could get me now. There was nowhere to run. The dome-covered terrace opened only to the aircraft landing platform.

"Now be a good human," Hezer gritted through his teeth, "and do as I say."

I panted, struggling to catch my breath after the mad dash through the lab.

"Will you really put your entire life's work and your good reputation on the line for this?" I kept retreating along the landing platform.

The night breeze caught the hem of my gown, playing with the loose strands of my hair. If I climbed into the aircraft, they'd easily open it and drag me out. I really had no choice, cornered and pushed against the edge of the landing pad.

My heart raced. My lungs pinched with each shallow breath I took. Dull pain rolled through my stomach, spasming somewhere just below the belly button.

I gasped, gripping my side.

"Careful, Maya." Egus stretched his arm to me, then turned to Hezer. "You stressed her out, Hezer. If she goes into labor now, we risk losing the baby."

Hezer only smirked, his eyes sparkling with anticipation. "What a great setback in Thormus's study that would be. We'd also get to examine the fetal matter that he'd never get his hands on."

The fetal matter?

Repulsion shuddered through me, head to toe.

"You'll end up in jail, you assholes!" I yelled.

Hezer didn't look concerned, however.

"Egus has an excellent system to dispose of lab waste, including cadavers."

My insides spasmed in horror. That would be all I would become after they were done with me—a cadaver.

"Maya," Egus shook his head with a mournful expression. "It didn't have to be like this."

"No, it didn't," I spat his way. "Had you been a decent man, none of this would have happened. But here we are."

He pressed both his hands to his chest, as if my words had wounded him. "We can still fix this. If you just do what we say—"

"If I do what you say," I finished for him, "you'll get whatever you want from me before killing me and quietly disposing of my body. But I can make it much more difficult for you to cover up my murder."

I grabbed the frame of the opening in the glass dome and climbed onto the ledge outside of it.

"Maya, no!" Egus screamed in distress.

Hezer shook his head, his eyes widening. "Stupid human."

Chapter 22

Maya

Aside from the landing platform, the glass dome covered the entire rooftop terrace, with only a thin ledge running along its circumference on the outside. It was barely wide enough to place my foot on.

Arching my back to press as much of my body as possible to the glass of the dome behind me, I shifted along the ledge away from the opening into the parking platform.

"Maya!" Egus shouted, leaning around the frame and stretching his arm to me.

I shuffled farther along the ledge and out of his reach. The wind blew stronger up here, tearing at the skirt of my long dress and tossing the strands of my hair into my face.

"You'll fall, stupid woman," Hezer warned, peeking from around Egus's shoulder. "And you'll die, splattered on the pavement stones below."

It'd be a long fall down from this height.

My pregnant belly considerably shifted my point of balance. I didn't dare bend forward to look down. Instead, I leaned back, pressing my shoulder blades into the glass of the dome behind me.

"My fall would mess up your plans, wouldn't it?" I willed my voice not to shake, screaming over the wind. "Scraping my dead body off the pavement in public view would make it harder to hide what you two assholes have done."

Despite my snappy reply, horror chilled me. I couldn't dwell on it, though. Any weakness on my part risked sending me down into the abyss. If my knees shook, if my foot slipped, I'd plummet to my death. There'd be no surviving a fall from this height.

"Maya, please." Egus's voice trembled with tears. Where were all these emotions when he snatched me from the assembly? "Just take my hand and come back here. We won't harm you. I promise."

The look on Hezer's face told me Egus had no authority to make any promises. The moment I gave in, they would dissect me in every way possible, then discard me as a *cadaver*.

"Why should I believe you, Professor Egus? You've lied and tricked me before."

A spasm rolled through my belly. My breath stuck in my throat. The urge to bend over in pain threatened to send me off the ledge. Instead, I splayed my arms on the dome behind me, scraping my fingernails against the glass.

Something wasn't right with the baby, and there was only one person in the entire Universe who could reassure me. But he wasn't here. Our call had lasted barely a second. Was it enough for Kear to realize I'd been taken against my will, brought to this tower, and was in dire need of help?

I doubted it.

Yet he was my only hope now.

Kear

"FUCK IT!" HE GRABBED the controls of his aircraft.

Obeying the speed limit, as per its program, was way too slow for him right now. Hand-flying, he sped up, steering the aircraft to the part of the city that his AI had pin-pointed as the location of Maya's call.

She was in trouble. He could tell by the panic in her voice when she screamed his name. Unfortunately, that was all she'd managed to say before the call went dead. Trying to re-connect didn't work. He dreaded to think what might've happened to her.

The controls grew slick from sweat under his palms. Warnings blared from the speaker, announcing the unacceptable speed violation.

He'd never heard this sound before because he'd never violated anything in his life before now. It'd been natural for him to move along the groves of rules and laws, to stay within limits and follow a routine. He'd respected both the laws of nature and the laws of people, never crossing the line.

Yet he would break all rules and cross all lines for Maya.

Without a moment of hesitation, he increased the speed of the aircraft even further, pushing it to the limit.

An alarm whined from the control panel. The authorities had been notified of his violation.

Good.

If they followed him to Maya, all the better. As long as they didn't try to delay him.

Among the cacophony of noises made by the control panel, his tablet pinged. A red dot flashed on the white screen, indicating he was getting closer.

A tall tower rose among the low-rise buildings on the outskirts of the city. To his knowledge, the tower carried a utilitarian purpose, not a residential one. No one lived there. But according to the tablet, that was where Maya had called him from.

A pale light illuminated the dome on the top of the tower.

He slowed down the aircraft and took it around the dome in search of a landing platform.

Then he saw her.

Maya, his quiet, gentle, delicate Maya, stood on the ledge outside of the rooftop dome. Her green dress billowed in the wind. Her fingers gripped the glass without purchase. There was nothing to prevent her from plummeting to her death with a strong gust of wind.

His heart stilled, his limbs growing cold. His fingers turned to ice on the controls.

"Hold on, sweetheart," he murmured under his breath, as if she could hear him. "Just hold on, please. I'm coming."

Egus and Hezer reached for her from the edge of the landing platform. A scorching-hot bolt of anger exploded in his chest.

They took her! Put her in danger. Scared her enough to send her onto the ledge.

How dare they!

He killed the engine before the aircraft came to a complete stop before it even touched the fake grass of the landing platform. He opened the door and leaped out of the seat.

"Thormus?" Hezer noticed him first as Egus was too preoccupied with coaxing Maya into taking his hand. "How the fuck—"

Kear planted his fist into Hezer's jaw, cutting off his question. Hezer stumbled back. He didn't look surprised at the attack. He knew he deserved it.

Hezer grabbed the nearest flowerpot filled with dirt and dead plants. Clearly, maintenance was not a priority in this place.

"Get out of the way!" Hezer lifted the heavy pot over his head.

Kear ducked, kicking a leg out. His left hoof shoved Hezer in the chest with force, knocking the air out of him. He tripped, falling backwards and dropping the flowerpot. Kear caught the pot in the air and pivoted around. Egus squeaked behind him, leaping for the door with impressive speed. Kear couldn't let him escape.

"Not so fast." Swinging the flowerpot, he tossed it after the traitor.

The heavy pot hit Egus between the shoulder blades, sending him to the ground, face first.

Hezer struggled to his hooves, but Kear shoved him back to the floor.

"You're not going anywhere, either," he gritted through his teeth.

He ripped Hezer's coat off, then yanked his shirt down his shoulders, using the sleeves to tie Hezer's wrists together. He then tied the ends of the shirt over the man's hooves, trussing him up like poultry ready for roasting.

"Thormus, listen..." Hezer struggled against the restraints. Only there was no use. Kear's knots had immobilized massive Ravil soldiers during surgeries he sometimes had been forced to perform on a battlefield without any pain medication to give them. "We can come to an agreement."

Kear scoffed. "What makes you think you're in any position to negotiate?"

He didn't wait for an answer. Grabbing Egus by the scruff of his coat, he tossed him inside his aircraft, then locked the door from the outside and disabled all controls.

"Maya." He rushed to the end of the platform and reached over the frame of the entrance to her. "Come here. Carefully."

Leaning all the way back, her head resting against the glass, she gave him a weak smile.

"Hezer lost on all fronts, didn't he? Not only is he behind you in research, but he sucks at kicking ass too."

He rubbed the soreness out of his knuckles. Never had he thought he'd use his combat skills after the war was over. But his rage for those two burned hotter than even his resentment toward his war enemies, *fescods*. It took all he had not to beat both Egus and Hezer to a pulp, lift them on his horns, then toss them off this fucking tower.

But Maya was still in danger, standing on the narrow ledge over the abyss.

Her face suddenly crumbled into a grimace of pain.

"Maya?" He placed a hoof onto the ledge. It slipped on the smooth surface.

Climbing after her made little sense. He'd just subject her to a higher risk of falling with him. He had to let her make her own way back to safety.

"Can you move toward me?" He beckoned with his hand.

She bit her lip, shutting her eyes tightly in the way-too-familiar expression. He'd delivered enough babies to recognize the face of a woman in labor. Panic shot through his chest with chilling sensation. He gripped the metal frame of the opening in the dome and leaned toward her as far as he could, risking falling out.

"Breathe, Maya," he said gently but firmly enough for his voice to cover the noise of the wind. "Don't move for now. Just count your breaths with me. One..."

He watched her chest expand, inhaling a quick, shallow breath.

"Good girl," he murmured. "Now, two..."

"Don't move," rushed through his head. *"Keep your legs strong. Lock your knees. Don't bend over. Don't fall... Please, please, please my sweet, dearest flower, don't fall."*

The begging in his head was pure panic. He couldn't let any of that slip through. For her sake, he had to keep calm or at least pretend convincingly enough that he was.

"It hurts," she groaned.

She could speak again. That was good. She could breathe. But she was going into early labor, standing on a narrow ledge over the city.

Terror twisted like a sharp blade in his chest, cutting his insides with cold, sickening fear.

Her breaths deepened. She gasped for air in the wind. The contraction must've ended, but a new one would come. He needed to do something quickly, while she could still hear him and follow his instructions.

"Maya, listen, don't make any sudden movements, but try to slide your left foot toward me. Don't take a step. Just a small, careful shuffle my way."

She nodded, drawing a shuddering breath in. Slowly, ever so slowly, she slid her left foot along the ledge, then jerkily followed the movement with her right one.

"Good…" He grasped for her, but she was still out of his reach. His hands came back empty. "A little more, Maya. Keep your palms on the glass. Your back, too."

He tore his gaze from her feet and met her eyes. They were darker than ever and opened so wide, he could see the whites all around her irises. She was terrified and in pain. Yet she held steady, slowly shifting closer to him.

He hated to think about what Egus and Hezer had done to send her to the ledge. Getting her back to safety was his priority. Otherwise, he'd wring their heads off their shoulders right that moment.

"You're doing great, Maya," he croaked. His throat was dry, and his hands sweaty. His heart thundered so loud, he could barely hear himself speak. "You're doing simply amazing, my brave, beautiful girl."

She shifted just a little closer, and he was able to grab her hand at last. Her fingers were as cold as ice. He gripped them in his, but didn't dare pull her to him, afraid she'd lose her balance.

"Almost there, Maya." His voice sounded exaggeratingly upbeat, cheering for every tiny progress she made in his direction. "A little closer…"

The moment he could trust getting a good hold of her, he grabbed her around the middle, then hauled her onto the landing platform. His legs shook, sending him to the ground with his treasure in his arms.

"I've got you," he exhaled. Relief flooded his muscles in a current so strong, he momentarily forgot how to breathe. "I've got you," he repeated, letting the thought sink in.

He had her. She didn't fall. She wasn't lying on the hard stones far below. He had her in his arms.

"You're crushing me," she mumbled into the fur above his neckline.

"Sorry." He laid her carefully across his lap, as if he were handling a precious, fragile jewel. Only Maya was much more precious to him than any jewels in the Universe. Somehow, she had become the most precious person in his life.

She gripped his hand with a groan. Another wave of pain must be rolling through her. He splayed a hand on her belly. It hardened under his palm with a contraction. She was in labor, and he had no equipment to monitor her condition, nothing to help her pain or to intervene if something went wrong.

"Kear," she squeezed his hand harder, "I'm scared."

He was scared, too. Terrified out of his wits. But he couldn't tell her that. He was all she had, and she needed him.

"It'll be fine, sweetheart." By some miracle, his voice managed to hide his panic, coming out impressively strong and confident. "I'm here."

But he was the only one here. The authorities, who he'd hoped would be right behind him, were still nowhere in sight. He feared he had no time to get her to the clinic on his own. The baby was coming, and he'd rather deliver her here on solid ground than in his aircraft on the way to the clinic, risking a crash.

Fear racked him. Cold paralyzing terror stilled his hands and impeded his thinking.

He tried to distance his mind from emotions and let the practical, calculating part of his brain do its job. It helped to view a patient as simply a body with a collection of organs for him to work on rather than a breathing, thinking, suffering being with a life to lose if he made a mistake. He'd often employed this mental tactic both during the war and in his clinic. It helped him keep a cool head and a steady hand when needed the most.

However, distancing wasn't easy this time. So much hinged on this woman. Not just his career, but his heart and his own life.

In just a few months, Maya had become his everything. Losing her was unthinkable. What harmed her pained him. He'd much rather have his own insides cut open and rearranged than have Maya go through any pain at all.

But she needed him. There was no one else in the entire Universe who knew her better than him or who could help her more than he could.

"Kear?" Her dark-as-night eyes searched his. Her fingers trembled as she curled them into his shirt. "We need to go to the hospital."

He drew in a long breath, calming his nerves for her sake. After gently laying her down on the fake grass of the landing platform, he ripped off his suit coat. Balling it into a bundle, he fitted it under her head instead of a pillow.

"Do you know why people rush to the hospital when they're in labor, Maya?" He gently tucked a strand of her hair behind her ear. "They go there to find *me*, so that I can help them. Out of every person in existence, I am the one you want here right now." He opened the cuffs of his sleeves, then rolled them up past his elbows. "You don't need to rush anywhere. Because I'm already with you, and I'm not going anywhere."

He cleaned his hands with the sanitary wipes he always carried with him. Sure, having his clinic's state-of-the-art equipment made his job easier. But it was his skills that made any equipment useful.

His hands and his brain were the most important tools he needed.

Gently prodding her belly, he confirmed the position of the baby. Bending her legs for her, he moved her long skirt out of the way.

When she looked at him again, fear had eased from her expression, making space for trust. He gave her a reassuring smile.

"I've got you, my flower, and I'm not letting you go. I promise, I'll keep you safe."

She was no longer clinging to the ledge over the abyss. Her life was in his hands now. And he'd be damned if he let any harm happen to her.

Chapter 23

Maya

I was lost in an ocean of pain. Swells rolled through me, one after another. Kear's voice guided me through each and every one of them.

"Breathe, Maya. Count the breaths with me." When the pain ebbed and the pressure eased, he'd ask random questions. "Why do you like purple? What Voranian food is your favorite? Tell me about the last holiday with your family."

The questions were annoying. Irritating. Maddening. But focusing on the answers took my mind off the pain. At that moment, I preferred irritation to the dread of waiting for another swell of agony to hit. Lying on my back seemed to make the pain stronger, all-consuming.

"I need to move." I gripped Kear's hand.

He helped me up, supporting me as I shuffled across the landing pad. My gaze crossed with Hezer's glower. Trussed up like a turkey, he scowled at me.

The echo of the latest contraction didn't stop my giggle.

"I bet you wish you had that combat training now," I gloated.

Kear chuckled, soothingly rubbing my back. "He wouldn't have made it through a single day of training."

Hezer spat a curse through his teeth. But his words drowned in the noise of two approaching aircraft.

"Finally," Kear exhaled as one landed nearby, the other one remained hovering over the dome.

A Voranian man dressed in the uniform of a law enforcement officer hopped out of the landed aircraft.

"Professor Thormus? A speed violation has been reported..." His voice trailed off as he took in the scene on the landing platform. Hezer, tied like a hog. Me, bent over in pain, clutching my belly. Egus banging on the glass of Kear's aircraft from the inside. "Is everything alright?" the officer asked uncertainly.

"Not even close," Kear snapped. "Get these two clowns out of here. They're guilty of far more violations than you could ever charge *me* with. And get my tablet out of my aircraft while you're at it, will you? The rest can be dealt with later, after we get the most important Voranian baby safely out of the most precious-to-me woman."

MY PREGNANCY LASTED for eight and a half months. The labor seemed to be taking twice as long. As pain came and ebbed, reality filtered through to me in blurry images.

At some point, an aircraft arrived and took Kear and me to the clinic. The entire team was already there, along with a bunch of other people I didn't know. Kear organized them all with brief but forceful commands.

I was brought into the delivery room and laid on the raised hospital bed. By then, I was so tired, my legs wouldn't hold me to keep walking around.

"Not long now," Kear assured me as the technicians strapped wires and monitors all over my body.

The pain finally seemed muffled somewhat. Someone must have given me something for it.

Kear fussed over me. His voice, clipped and commanding with the others, turned to gentle cooing when he spoke to me.

"You're doing great, Maya. You're brave and strong. So strong, my beautiful girl."

I didn't feel strong. My legs shook. My vision swam. I just wanted to curl into myself and sleep for a few months or so. The only thing that seemed wide awake was my mouth. The longer the labor took, the angrier I felt, and the more vocal I became.

"Ugrrr," I groaned through yet another contraction. The whole world seemed to be reduced to the endless tide of pressure and pain. "Get this thing out of me, Kear. Now!"

The sweet little baby that I willingly grew in my belly for months, getting along with it just fine, had now become "this thing" I couldn't wait to be rid of because that seemed the one and only way to finally stop this torture.

"Use those fucking muscles of yours," I gritted through my teeth, bracing for another swell of pressure, "and pull that thing out. You put it in, you get it out."

"Not long now, dearest." He smiled at my verbal abuse, probably just happy that I was still alive and kicking.

One thing I no longer felt was fear.

Even when the foreheads of his assistants wrinkled in worry, Kear remained calm and in control. His confidence gave me strength, for which I was grateful. Despite his earlier lies and deception, I trusted his promise to keep me safe.

At the end, he did use his muscles, literally. A suction cup was attached to the baby's head, and Kear pulled it out by a rope in a rather primitive looking fashion. His arm muscles bunched up with strain against the resistance of the baby stuck in my birth canal. He pulled gently but steadily.

A tiny wail shrilled through the bustling activity in the room, and I knew it was finally over.

The pressure eased momentarily. The pain dulled to a faint shadow of its former self. I drew in my first deep breath in what felt like centuries.

"Are the parents here?" I croaked, feeling like I'd just run a marathon, with a bucket of rocks tied to my middle.

I had no idea how long it all took or even what time of the day it was. But something significant had just happened in the life of a couple who had put their trust and hopes in me. I expected the parents of the baby to burst into the room. They surely had been pacing outside the door all this time, overwhelmed by hope and worry.

All I wanted after all this torture was to see the smiles on their faces as they held their baby for the first time.

The room went still. Other than for the team of pediatricians busying themselves over the baby's miniature bed under a lamp dome, no one moved. Nobody burst through the door, eager to see their new child.

"She is perfect," a pediatrician announced.

She.

My face split with a smile so wide, my cheeks felt sore. "It's a girl?"

"Congratulations, Professor Thormus." The pediatrician put the tiny bundle into Kear's arms.

He froze. His breathing halted as he looked down at the baby. He blinked rapidly, tilting his head. His eyes studied the baby's face intently. The veil of confidence wavered, giving way to vulnerability in his expression.

I realized the pediatrician didn't just congratulate a renowned professor on a successful completion of the most important study of his career. He congratulated the father on the birth of his child.

"She's yours?" I exhaled.

He nodded, not taking his eyes off his daughter's face, scrunched into a grimace to accompany her wailing scream.

"*Just* yours?" I clarified.

He nodded again. "The egg came from an anonymous donor."

There was no mother. No happy couple, waiting impatiently to claim their baby. All this little girl had was Kear.

But he turned around, handing the baby to one of his assistants. "Situate her into the capsule for observation."

She, just like me, was nothing more but a subject of his study.

As two nurses cleaned me, Kear faced me again.

"You will stay in bed until the end of today. We'll assess your status in the morning." He stepped closer and placed a hand on my shoulder. He was wearing gloves, and his touch reminded me of the many medical tests he'd performed on me. "How are you feeling, Maya?"

I stared straight ahead at the horns of one of the nurses who were changing the sheets under me and tucking clean covers around me.

"You know exactly how I'm feeling, Professor." I tipped my chin at the walls of monitors surrounding my bed. Every aspect of my physical existence was scrupulously documented and displayed in the neat charts and graphs for him to see.

He squeezed my shoulder slightly. "That's not what I meant."

"What else could you mean? What else really matters to you?" I drew in a breath and finally looked up at him. "It's over now. The results of your precious study no longer hinge on my wellbeing. You no longer need to pretend you care. No need to lie or go through the trouble of forging someone else's letters."

He signed so heavily, his chest vibrated with a growl.

"Maya—"

"It's Madam Maya Gupta to you, Professor Thormus. It's what it always should have been."

"Maya... Please." He pressed both hands into the mattress, leaning over me. "It has never been just about the study—"

"Never?" I narrowed my eyes at him.

"Well..." He rubbed his forehead. "At the very beginning, yes. Maybe."

"At the beginning, in the middle, and at the end. It has always been the biggest thing you cared about. The *only* thing."

"No." He shook his head.

I lifted a hand, stopping his argument. "That's fine. Really. You are what you are. Work is and always has been the most important part of your life. It's a good, noble kind of work. I actually admire you for what you do. What I hate is that you would throw everything under the wheels of your ambition."

"That's not true!" He pushed back from the bed.

The nurses finished cleaning me and joined the rest of the men who congregated by the opposite wall. They looked unsure whether to leave the room and give us privacy or stick around in case a fight broke out and they had to tear us apart to stop us from clawing each other's eyes out.

"Not true? Really?" I huffed a humorless laugh. "But what is your exact definition of truth, Professor? To my knowledge, you have no clue what truth is."

"Maya, please listen to me. I care about you more than anything in the world. Nothing is more important to me... The work... I— Ughh," he groaned, fisting his hands in frustration. "I'm not good with words."

"*That* is not true. I've read some wonderful words written by you that were simply magical. They helped me through some very hard times. Or were all those words stolen from someone else, just like the signature you stole from Walter?"

"I didn't steal anything." His cheeks darkened in a blush. His eyes glistened in agitation. "I tried, but the words of others didn't work."

"Can't say I'm sorry about that, or that I'm sorry for you." I felt winded and weak. Every sound released from my mouth robbed me of energy. "You've done what you had to do here, Professor. Now, please leave."

He stomped his hoof in determination. His tail lashed out, hitting the screen stands with so much force they shook.

"I'm not going anywhere."

"I'm tired, Professor. Leave me alone," I said firmly, sinking into the puffy cushions of my bed. "Go to your daughter. She needs you. The poor thing had the misfortune of getting you for a parent. She has no one else."

Chapter 24

Kear

It was best to stay busy. Bombarded with a flurry of activities, he had no time to think or to *feel*.

So many things had to be done. The long study reached the most fantastic conclusion—a baby was born. Both his subjects fared well. Data had been collected and organized, with preliminary findings shared at the assembly.

On top of that, the authorities requested his and Maya's reports about the ordeal with Egus and Hezer. He tried to shield her from that as much as he could, dealing with them on his own whenever possible.

The research data of Hezer and Egus was seized and analyzed. It turned out that in their effort to beat him, the two had used not just unethical but also illegal practices. For that and for what they did to Maya, the two crooks were heading to jail for the rest of their lives.

Once all these activities had slowed down, however, Kear was left one on one with his thoughts and feelings.

Maya requested a transfer from the hospital. Alcus Hecear, the nice man that he was, immediately moved her to an apartment in the building that belonged to the Liaison Committee. Kear had no power to stop him. Maya had ceased to be under his authority, the moment the study was over.

As per Voranian custom, the baby joined the academy as soon as she was deemed physically well enough to leave the hospital. A staff of trained educators and infant caregivers was now taking care of her, with reports sent to him daily.

He didn't need to make much effort in raising his daughter, unless he wished to take her home on the weekends, which he would, except that she'd probably be better off with the professionals than with him. Despite all his experience in bringing babies into the world, he knew little about what to do with them after they were born.

Finally, Kear was left alone in his apartment, as he had always been. Only life was far from normal.

He now had human-Voranian couples lining up to use his method for starting their families. He had fame, more money than he knew what to do with, and the opportunity to continue his work for as long as he wished.

But nothing felt the way it should. The silence in his place was normal, but the space rang with loneliness, which was unwelcome and depressing.

He knew where Maya was, but she didn't want to see him. He wasn't even sure how long she was planning to stay in Voran. He'd contacted Representative Alcus Hecear and extended an official invitation for Maya to stay on the planet indefinitely at Kear's personal expense. The Governor would approve her stay as a gesture of gratitude from the country. Maya was sort of a celebrity now, with a special status in Voran. But no matter how many times he'd called Alcus since, the representative could not confirm that she accepted his offer. He feared she never would.

Nothing held her in Voran. She'd made no friends here. Kear had made it difficult for her to meet people by limiting her interactions outside of the study. She could leave any day, and he would never see her again.

The notion twisted in his chest with never ending sorrow.

He'd called the Liaison Committee building so many times, he could swear even his AI drone got tired from connecting the same number over and over again. But she refused to speak with him, declining all his calls.

Maybe she'd be better off without him?

"You have no clue what truth is."

Her words had stung when she'd said them. And they still hurt. But she was right, he had lied to her.

When he did it, he honestly believed it was in her best interests. He only wished to postpone the pain and suffering of the breakup with her good-for-nothing boyfriend. He hadn't realized until much later that by doing so, he'd ultimately added to her pain.

In the end, his actions had turned out to be just as bad as those of the human who'd wronged her. Kear was an asshole, just like Walter. They both had lied to Maya.

"I've read some wonderful words written by you," she'd said. *"Or were they all stolen?"*

He had lied to her. But not to the extent she believed he did.

Yes, he sent his letters to her through the account of her ex-boyfriend, leading her to believe they were from him. But the words he wrote were his. Every single one of them.

He stopped at his desk, hands propped on the smooth surface. One of the screens of his research device flickered to life. He opened his personal correspondence.

The phrases he'd tried to steal when writing that first love letter to her popped on the screen. The words in Maya's language glowed like squared worms, incomprehensible to his eyes.

"Read out loud," he ordered the AI.

"I'll die for you."

"I can't live without you."

"You complete me…"

They all used to sound like utter gibberish to him before. Now, their meaning emerged sharply, as if the fog shrouding his mind had cleared.

Yes, he would die for Maya with no hesitation. He wished it would've been him standing on that ledge instead of her. It'd be far less stressful than seeing her in danger.

No, he couldn't live without her. If she left Neron now, he would survive. He'd go through the motions. He'd take care of his daughter. He'd do his work. He'd survive, but that would not be the life he'd want to have. Without Maya, he couldn't be happy. He'd survive, but he couldn't *live* fully.

Because she did *complete* him.

There was a hole the size of a human woman in his heart now. And only she could fill it.

"Fuck," he groaned, dropping his head between his shoulders.

He was truly and utterly fucked, wasn't he?

He was in love.

"I love her, don't I?" he asked the screen. The AI remained silent and, in this case, completely useless.

He loved Maya. And he was about to lose her.

His first instinct was to run to her. Except that she no longer lived in the hospital. Chances were, she'd refuse to see him. But even if she didn't, there was a huge possibility he'd screw it up even more the moment he opened his mouth. Being in the same room with her robbed him of words. Thoughts deserted him, making him feel light-headed and dumb.

If he went to her, he'd ruin it.

"I've read some wonderful words written by you..."

He was good with words. But in this case, he was only good when the words were written. He'd composed some beautiful love letters to her, expressing the emotions he'd never thought himself capable of. Because all those words had come straight from his heart.

Maya used to love his letters. Maybe he could make her love them again. And through them, maybe he'd get a second chance at her love, too?

This time, he'd also get to put his own name under the words expressing his feelings.

"To Madam Maya Gupta," he dictated to the AI. Then, he closed his eyes and let his heart speak once again. The words flowed easily, "Maya, my dearest beautiful flower..."

Chapter 25

Maya

Holding my tablet in both hands, I stared at Kear's letter. It came from his account and was written in Voranian. To understand it, I had to have my room's AI read it out loud for my translator to convert it to English.

Though, I believed I shouldn't do it.

Logic told me it'd be easier to make a nice clean cut in our relationship, whatever that had been. I'd started by moving out of his clinic where nearly every wall and every door bore a sign with his name. I didn't even need to have it read to me. I'd learned to recognize his name in writing.

To complete the "nice clean cut" I should leave the planet. The study was finished two weeks ago. My contract was done. The payment had long been transferred to me. Yet here I was, lingering on Neron for no apparent reason.

I told myself I had to see more of Voran before leaving it for good. In the past week, I'd gone to a few museums, visited the zoo, met several human women married to Voranian men to chat about their life here on the new planet. I'd even taken a day trip to the countryside, to get the full experience. Yet I couldn't bring myself to confirm a seat on the next spaceship leaving for Earth.

Something held me back.

Well, maybe reading this letter would release me from whatever it was.

I drew in a full chest of air, then exhaled it with one word, "Read."

"Maya, my dearest beautiful flower," the AI droned, but in my mind, Kear's deep, rambling voice took over. *"I hope with all my heart that you will read this letter because this is the best way I can explain myself to you. And I do need to explain everything that happened. I have to try to make you understand.*

I love you..."

"Wait," I choked out, stopping the AI. "What?"

"I love you," the robotic voice repeated dutifully.

"He couldn't... He...just..." My head was spinning, refusing to produce a single cohesive thought.

"Do you wish to proceed?" the AI inquired.

"Yes." I nodded, holding my breath. "Please."

People didn't lie to those they loved. And if they did, it wasn't true love. It was manipulation. His confession meant nothing. It couldn't change anything.

"I'm sorry, Maya. I'm so sorry I hurt you." Kear's words continued to fill the room. *"I was stupid, clueless, and naïve when I took over your correspondence with Walter. I didn't even realize that by doing it, I'd be playing with feelings I knew nothing about.*

But my intentions weren't evil. I didn't set out to deceive or destroy you. I merely believed I'd be helping you..."

Helping?

An incredulous laugh scraped inside my throat.

Could a grown man really be that *clueless?*

He did it out of concern for his study. Everything Kear had ever done was motivated by that. If he didn't see it, then he was lying to himself, too.

"I admit, my initial motivation to keep you safe and happy came from the concern for my work and the final result of the study. I also had no idea how to communicate with a woman outside of a strictly professional relationship. So, I did try to steal some words and to research how to write romantic letters..."

Of course he did. Where else would all those beautiful words come from? Deep inside I always knew they were too good, even for Walter, who'd been with me for a decade and knew me better than Kear did. No way Kear could've composed letters like that on his own. He'd never dated before. Never cared for anyone. He couldn't possibly love me. Those words must be stolen too.

"But that particular research failed me. You see, Maya, the only way a love letter can sound real is if every word of it is felt. It has to come from a living, beating heart of a person capable of feeling, even if those feelings hurt.

So no, I didn't steal or borrow the words I wrote to you. They were all mine and only mine. I used Walter's account, but after a couple of tries, I couldn't even bring myself to put his name on the letters I wrote to you. It was a candid conversation between you and me, and no one else.

I love you, Maya.

You are the only woman I have ever loved, and the only one I'll ever love for the rest of my days.

If you choose to leave, I can't stop you. But I wish, pray, and hope that you will stay. Because I no longer can imagine my life without you.

Our correspondence can never stop. The conversation I started months ago will forever continue whether you're near me or not. I speak with you daily. In my mind, I keep telling you about my day. I share my thoughts and feelings with you and only you.

This is my reality now. You've made your way so deep into my life, my thoughts, and my very being that there is no way to separate me from you anymore.

You are a part of me, and I'd do anything to keep us whole.

Please give me a chance to right the wrong. Stay. Give me some time to prove to you that you already know me, all of me. You know me better than anyone in the Universe. I hid nothing from you. You just have to put the right name on the person behind the letters.

I hope you read this because I can never put accurately everything I feel into words when I speak to you.

I hope you'll reply.

I'll be waiting.

I live for your letters. Even if this is the last one I'll ever get to write to you.

With all my love. Kear."

A tear fell on the screen. I quickly brushed off another one from my cheek. For someone who claimed he was bad with words, he seemed to find some pretty good ones every time.

The best word this time was his name at the end. It was like a ray of honesty in the fog of deception that had been surrounding me. I wondered how he felt signing with his own name for once.

I had no idea how to feel about all of this now.

How much of what he wrote was true? Could I even trust him? After all, he'd been lying to me for months.

I opened the folder with the vast collection of all his letters, all that came from Walter's account.

It was easy to find the one when Kear hijacked our correspondence and took over. The first letter he wrote was much shorter and sounded far more reserved. It was signed *"Walter."* The name looked like a mockery to me, blinking at me from the screen like a cruel joke.

I remembered how I felt the day I received it. I was relieved that Walter had reconsidered breaking up with me, but I also felt confused. Walter didn't sound like him in this one. He didn't sound like Walter in any that came after this one, either.

In them, he sounded better. More considerate, selfless, caring. He sounded like the friend that Walter might've been to me at some point at the beginning of our relationship but hadn't been for some time at the end.

No wonder I'd accepted the deception so easily. I *wanted* to believe Walter was back. That I had a friend once again. And in a way, I did have a friend. Walter never wrote these letters, but they gave me the support I so badly needed.

I kept opening the letters, scrolling through them one by one and remembering all the warm feelings they had caused when I'd first read them.

After the first two, none of the other ones were signed with Walter's name. There was no name at all. Instead of a signature, there were just short phrases of encouragement, support, and affection that grew increasingly warmer and brighter as time went by.

There were no silly nicknames that Walter liked to use, none of his usual mannerisms. Kear had made no effort to sound like my ex. As I re-read his letters, the words sounded in his voice in my head.

They were his all along.

Walter never spoke like this. But Kear did.

How could I not see it earlier?

In a way, I believed I did see it. I sensed some dissonance. But I attributed it to Walter's changing and becoming more mature. It was easy enough to believe the changes in him since I hadn't seen him for over a year.

I stopped scrolling and dropped my face into my hands.

What was I to do now?

"*I love you,*" Kear's words echoed in my head.

But were they true?

Would I be stupidly setting myself up for another heartbreak if I believed them?

Or would I make the biggest mistake of my life if I didn't?

I glanced at the Voranian characters at the end of Kear's letter. I believed those meant "*I hope you'll reply.*"

I hit the reply button and typed.

"Summer is beautiful in Voran. I've decided to take a few days to enjoy it before returning to Earth. After two weeks of sightseeing, however, I believe I've seen all I wanted to see except for one thing.

Back in the hospital I watched a lot of documentaries about Aldraian gardening technique. Did you know they have trees on the planet Aldrai big enough to use as houses? There is one in Victory Park just outside of the City of Voran, and I want to see it before I leave this planet. I'm going to the park this weekend to take a tour. If the weather is as nice as they forecast it to be, I'll be having lunch in the park, too."

After a moment of consideration, I added, *"Victory Park is a great place to bring a baby."*

If he showed up, it'd be a great opportunity to see them both, either to figure things out or at least to say goodbye.

Alcus Hecear was waiting for me to confirm my departure date for Earth. Either way, I should be in the position to finally do it after my trip to Victory Park tomorrow.

Chapter 26

Maya

The *bhicut* tree looked like an entire forest up close. Its roots rose from the ground, taking up an area the size of a city block from back home. Each root was as big as a tree trunk, and there were probably a hundred of them. They grew straight up, connecting into arches high above my head and forming the main trunk of the giant tree.

I followed the group of out-of-town tourists that weaved between the roots under the tree.

Our tour-guide drone hovered over the crowd, relaying facts and statistics about the magnificent tree.

"Though this species is quite common in some parts of the planet Aldrai, it is the only one of its kind on Neron. The tree was a gift from Aldrai to Neron to commemorate a major trade agreement signed a hundred and fifteen years ago between the two planets," the drone informed us.

I spotted a large orange flower on the vine twining up one of the roots and stopped to smell it. The "flower" trembled, its "petals" closed into a bud, then opened again like an umbrella. The creature separated from the vine and flew up with a faint buzzing noise.

I gasped in surprise, jumping back.

"The tree creates its own ecological mini system," the drone continued. "Twenty-seven life forms have been exported from Aldrai to live among its roots and up in its canopy. Unable to survive in the environment outside of the tree, the exported species remain in its proximity, thus not threatening the existing biosystems on Neron."

Without touching or sniffing this time, I studied the colorful plumes and rosettes peppering the vines around the roots. I tried to guess which ones were flowers and which might be insects or other small creatures.

"Fascinating," I muttered under my breath. The tree looked even more alien to me than the alien planet I was on. "Aldrai must be a gorgeous place."

"It is," the familiar deep voice said behind me.

I pivoted around, coming face to face with Kear.

He cleared his throat, awkwardly shifting his weight to another hoof.

"Aldraians put a lot of effort into beautifying their planet," he said stiffly. "It's definitely worth a visit."

"Oh..." I blinked, his awkwardness seeping into my muscles too. "Have you been to Aldrai?"

"Yes. Once. For a conference."

"I see." I nodded, trying to reconcile the famous Professor Thormus with the man from "Walter's" letters, and with Kear, the friend I thought I had during the past months of my pregnancy.

It wasn't easy to think about all of them as one person. Especially since the man standing in front of me now didn't even look like any of them.

His sandy beige pants were wrinkled. There was a wet stain on his left shoulder. He must have missed the last appointment at the barber because the fur on his head looked overgrown and uncharacteristically messy. His beard had grown longer, too.

The Professor Thormus I knew would've never shown up in public like this. Still, my heart skipped a beat at the sight of him.

I missed him and our conversations, in letters and otherwise.

"Sorry, we're late. I tried to get here before the start of the tour, but...things took longer than I'd planned." He patted a small bundle attached to his chest by a wide, soft harness.

I gaped at the tiny tuft of pale-gray fur sticking out of the harness. "Is that the baby?"

He nodded with a smile. A small wagon hovered at his side with a padded bassinet inside and a wicker basket with a lid.

"She's thriving in the academy, but I've heard Victory Park is a great place to take a baby." He echoed the words from my letter. "So, I brought her home for the weekend."

"Good. I'm glad you did."

It was good to see them together. I knew my role in his baby's life ended with her birth. But after "housing" that little girl for so long, I wished her only the best outside of my womb, too. Back at the hospital, it'd pained me to see that the person who was supposed to be the closest to her didn't seem to want to be close to her at all. His efforts now made me feel slightly more optimistic about their future together.

"Do you want to join me on the tour, Professor? It won't take long. It's almost over."

"*Kear.* Please call me Kear, Maya."

It sounded almost like an introduction, like we'd just met for the first time. And maybe that was how I should look at it—a start from scratch. A new beginning? Or at the very least, closure with an amicable parting at the end.

He walked alongside me, following the drone. The tour ended in a few minutes. But that was enough time for me to deal with my anxiety. He also looked a little more at ease as we exited from under the tree and into the park.

The baby woke up, squirming in the carrier.

"She must be hungry." He smiled apologetically.

"I'm getting hungry, too," I said. "There is a café at the entrance."

"Or we can have a picnic." He pointed at the basket and laughed. "That is if you don't mind eating the hospital food again."

He brought a picnic for us. I found it endearing enough even to eat the hospital food again.

I tilted my head. "Did you only bring things that are on the list of the approved foods?"

"No. I gravely violated the rules. I even packed some dessert."

Now, I was laughing, too.

"I'm all for that kind of violation!"

We found a nice spot under a much smaller, locally grown tree away from the main path of the park. I helped him spread two self-inflating cushions for us to sit on. He took out a round sphere with milk from the basket, then adjusted his daughter at his chest.

I stole little glances at the baby. Her pale-gray fur looked soft and downy on her head but so short on her face, the sun cast a sheen on her tiny button nose and her high Voranian cheekbones. The tiny buds of horns graced her forehead like two dark peas. I wished I could see the rest of her—the little hooves that kept kicking me from the inside only two weeks ago, the tail, and her belly. I wished I could hold her. But I didn't ask Kear to take her, reining in my instincts.

He turned the sphere with my breast milk in his fingers and fitted its nipple into the baby's mouth. She eagerly sucked on it.

My chest tingled as the baby nursed. The day she was born, I was asked to consider pumping my breast milk for her. I wasn't even sure how long I was going to stay on Voran, but I immediately agreed to do that. I'd been pumping twice a day, in the morning and at night. But this was the first time I got to see my efforts' final destination.

"What's her name?" I asked.

He took a suspiciously long time to answer before finally blurting out, "Anika."

I sucked in a breath, sitting back. "You took my grandmother's name."

He shot me a tentative glance. "Does it make you angry?"

"It depends. Why did you do it?"

He dropped his gaze to his daughter, watching her nurse.

"I..." His brows moved together in concentration. "I wanted her to have a stronger connection with you, even if neither of you knew about it."

"We're not supposed to have any connection after her birth. I was just a surrogate."

"I know. But I thought it would be nice for her to have something of yours. After you...*if* you left. She is the only Anika in this part of the Galaxy."

"The only Voranian baby with a human name," I added.

"And for now, the only Voranian baby grown in a human woman's womb." He peered at me again. "Are you angry about the name?"

I probably should be. But I didn't feel angry. Instead, sadness filtered into my heart at the thought of leaving them both soon. With the five-month-long journey between our planets, even visiting here didn't seem feasible.

Blinking the sadness away, I stared at the fluff of fur between the baby's little horns.

"She's adorable."

He nodded, holding the baby in a rather awkward position that probably made his arms sore.

"Why did you never tell me she was yours?"

He shifted uncomfortably.

"I didn't really tell anyone. Those who knew found out from the research paperwork that few people had access to."

"Why did you decide to become a father?"

"I didn't. I never planned for this to happen."

"What?" I stared at him incredulously. "How could you *not* have planned it? It's not like she's an accidental result of drunken night of passion."

He glanced aside. "No. She is the result of working late into the night, running out of frozen sperm specimens, and ending up using what I had...um, on hand, so to say."

"You used your own sperm in tests," I finished for him.

"Yes."

"You didn't think it would work?"

"At that stage, it shouldn't have. But that's when my lucky breakthrough happened. If I'd gone back and tried to recreate the results with a donor's sperm, it would've delayed me by months, if not years."

"So, you just kept going?"

He dropped his head, saying nothing.

A compassion for the baby fluttered inside me. I really wished she had parents, or at least a parent, who desperately wanted to have her from the very beginning and would love her with all their heart.

"How are you feeling about being a dad now, Kear?"

He adjusted the sphere meant to imitate a woman's breast in his hand, lifting it a little higher for a better flow. He appeared to do all the right things, but he looked more like a doctor doing them than a father.

"I'm fine with it," he said. "Why do you ask?"

"You're holding the baby so far away from your chest, one could fly an aircraft between you and her."

He took a critical look at their positions. "Her head is supported and her spine isn't strained."

"But don't you wish to cuddle her?" My hands itched to touch her. My skin tingled with the urge to cuddle that fuzzy little bundle, to nuzzle her fur and kiss her chubby cheeks, even when I knew I wasn't supposed to do any of those things. She wasn't mine. But she was all his to love and cherish unconditionally.

"I do cuddle her." He pointed at the harness crisscrossing his wide chest.

"But do you *wish* to do it? Do you like doing it? Or do you cuddle just because her teachers told you to?"

He looked down at his baby again. Oblivious to our discussion, she nursed peacefully, her pearly-gray eyelids fluttered closed.

"I am her parent," he said slowly, as if needing to hear it out loud himself. "I feed her, clothe her, pay for her education..."

I drew in a breath, disheartened. This wasn't what I hoped to hear. Baby Anika deserved so much more than being looked after purely out of obligation.

"But I also feel more protective of her than I've ever felt," he continued. "It's visceral, beyond any logic or my control. If anyone so much as looks at her the wrong way, I'd lift them on my horns and wring their neck without hesitation."

"Wow..." I blinked, impressed by the fierce conviction in his voice. "That's a start, I guess."

Baby Anika drifted to sleep, the imitation nipple slipping out of her mouth. Kear put her into the motorized wagon with the bassinet, then we ate lunch.

By that point, I was too hungry to be picky about the food. He'd brought a lot of healthy options, of course. Some pieces tasted less blunt than others, but overall, it brought back memories of all the hospital lunches we used to share.

Slowly, the awkwardness melted away. We chatted like before. Kear caught me up-to-date on how everyone on his team was doing. I told him about places I'd visited in the past week.

"Ready for dessert?" He asked, taking out the familiar pink box from his basket.

"Did you..." I gasped in delight. "Did you get me some cupcakes from Earth Girl's Desserts?"

He grinned.

"Well, they say these are the best cupcakes in this part of the Galaxy. They are also the *only* cupcakes in this part of the Galaxy, so..." He shrugged.

I grabbed one the moment he opened the box.

"Oh, so good." I hummed around a mouthful of deliciousness with appreciation. "You've got to try it."

I thrust my cupcake his way. He leaned closer and took a bite.

"It's good." He nodded. "Unbelievably sweet. But good."

A drop of pink frosting clung to his beard.

"You've got something here. Let me..." I reached for it before giving it a thought.

He stilled as I moved closer. I swiped the icing with my thumb and glanced up. His eyes were on me, searching. His familiar scent invaded my senses. The effect of his proximity seemed that much stronger because there was nothing standing between us this time. No Walter on my side, and no lies on his.

"How long are you planning to stay on Neron, Maya?" he asked softly and appeared to hold his breath waiting for my answer.

"I..." I cleared my throat, shifting away in need of some distance between us to be able to think clearly. "I haven't decided yet. There is a spaceship leaving for Earth the day after tomorrow, but I haven't confirmed with Alcus whether I want to be on it yet."

"What can I do to get you to stay longer?"

I stuffed another huge bite of cupcake into my mouth, just to give myself some time to think. After finishing the entire cupcake, I still had no definite answer to give him.

"I honestly don't know, Kear. On one hand, there is no rush for me to leave. On the other hand, I don't think I should linger, either, as not to...you know, prolong the inevitable."

Now that I got to see him again, leaving him seemed harder than ever. But should I be staying for a man who had deceived me so gravely?

I grabbed another cupcake in desperate hopes of eating away my dilemma and checked on Anika.

"She's sleeping so well." I changed the subject.

He exhaled a brief laugh. "During the day, she does."

"Not so much at night?"

He sighed, running his hand through the overgrown fur on his head. "At night, she woke up more times than I could count."

"Was she hungry?"

"She ate." He nodded. "But it's more than that. I think she just wants to play or socialize. She'd just be looking at me, wide awake, alert and happy."

That explained his disheveled appearance and the thick veil of exhaustion shrouding his eyes.

"She's so cute," I cooed, watching the baby. "So peaceful right now."

"Mhm." He smiled. "Hard to believe she could ever be a tool of torture."

After lunch, we strolled around the park a little. The bassinet with the sleeping baby silently flew over the ground next to Kear.

When it was time to leave, I walked him to the parking tower.

"I'll fly you back to the Liaison Committee's building," he offered.

The baby squirmed, making soft sleepy noises.

"It looks like she'll be up soon," I noted. "Do you have more milk?"

He checked, lifting the lid of the basket.

"Some." He sounded uncertain.

"Just go straight to the hospital, then. I was planning to take a taxi back to my building, anyway."

He paused at the bottom of the stairs that led up the tower with its many parking levels above.

"Maya. I don't want this to be the last time I see you."

His somber voice tugged at my heart with realization. I didn't want this to be my last time seeing him, either. But I was scared, so scared of another heartbreak. How many of those can one heart take?

Afraid to meet his eyes, I stared straight ahead at his chest instead.

"Kear, is what you wrote in your last letter true?"

"Every word." Taking my face in his hands, he lifted my head until our gazes collided. "I love you."

My heart thudded at hearing it from him out loud. Tenderness flooded my limbs with warmth.

"I love you, my beautiful flower," he repeated softly. "It was a sudden realization on my part, but one without any doubt. I never thought I'd ever fall in love. But here I am…" He spread his arms at his sides, as if offering himself to me. "I'm desperately in love with a woman who has every right to curse my name for eternity."

That'd be a sad and lonely eternity for both of us if I chose to hate him for that long.

I splayed a hand on his chest, just above the baby harness. My palm was cushioned by the thick fur under the soft material of his shirt. I took a step closer, and he met me half-way.

"Maya…" His eyes searched mine, saying even more than his words.

His face was so close to mine, just a heartbeat away from a kiss. I realized that as brilliant as this man was academically, he had absolutely no experience in romance or sex. If I wanted a kiss, I had to do it myself. I had to abandon my natural role as a follower and take the lead.

Sliding both my hands up his chest, I rose to my tiptoes and reached for his mouth with mine. His lips parted under my touch, but he didn't go much further. Maybe because he didn't know how.

Holding his head in my hands, I took his bottom lip between mine, kissing him gently. I did it slowly, giving us both time to adjust to this new intimacy between us.

He "adjusted" quickly, however. With a strangled groan, he grabbed me, tugging me to him so tightly, my feet lifted off the ground.

Deepening the kiss, he swallowed my gasp. His hand slid up my back, his fingers sinking into my hair on the back of my head. Even when he let me come up for air, he wouldn't remove his mouth from me, kissing my face, then the side of my neck. His breathing came in sharp, ragged puffs. The hard ridge of his erection grew, pressing against my thigh.

My head was spinning with giddiness. I wrapped my arms around his neck as he held me in a crushing embrace. Next to the stairs, we were out of view from the people strolling along the paths in the park, but anyone going to or from the parking platforms could witness our wonderfully messy make-out session that went way past the chaste kiss I'd first intended.

Reluctantly, I pulled back. My heart was racing in my chest. My face felt flushed. Kear's expression was unguarded, open, and raw.

I smoothed the fur over his forehead. "Ask me again how long I'm staying on Neron."

"How long?" he breathed out.

"I'll take the full month after Anika's birth. As per the contract."

His shoulders sagged with relief. "Two more weeks left, then."

"A little more than two weeks. We can have another date." I smiled, warm excitement tingling inside me like champagne bubbles. "If that's what you w—"

"Tomorrow," he blurted out before I even had a chance to finish. "Can I see you again tomorrow?"

"Tomorrow it is." My smile stretched so wide it could probably reach from here all the way back to Earth. "Now go, Kear. Before you scare all the passersby with that hard-on of yours. It's about to reach the size of this tower."

He leaned his head to mine, the base of his horns pressing gently on each side of my forehead.

"Tomorrow."

Chapter 27

Kear

It was at least an hour before he had to leave the hospital building to pick up Maya for their third date, but he was itching to see her right now.

"Call Maya," he ordered his house AI.

The large screen in his main living room blinked to life. Maya's face appeared on it a moment later.

"Hi, Kear." She smiled, brushing her hair. It was damp. A thin towel sheet was wrapped around her. She must've just had a shower, getting ready for their date. "Sorry, I'm not dressed yet."

Her smile turned teasing, and his cock jumped to attention. It was his own fault, he ambushed her with a call without warning.

She tilted her head, her eyes sliding down his frame from his freshly painted horns to his smoothly polished hooves. "You look completely ready, though. Aren't you a bit early?"

He shrugged, trying to downplay his obvious desperation. "I couldn't wait."

Throughout the day, he did his best to focus on his work, but the moment his brain was free from charts and formulas, all his thoughts immediately drifted to her.

She sat down in front of the mirror in her room. "You'll have to watch me getting ready, then. I still need a few minutes."

He'd watch her in anything she wished to do—getting ready, drying her hair, getting dressed... His eyes drifted to the towel sheet hugging her curves. He stared at it unblinking, wishing his gaze had the power to vaporize it.

"How was your day?" she asked innocently.

He tore his attention from the sheet and focused on her face instead as she rubbed some cream into her skin.

"Good." He cleared his throat, banishing his lustful thoughts. Though they would never leave him for long.

He wanted Maya more than anything, but it had to be on her terms. He had messed up so badly before, every step she took now had to be because she *wanted* to take it. He'd wait for her to come to him, even if it took a lifetime of atonement on his part.

"How about yours?" he asked.

"Oh, I had an excellent day!" she gushed. "I spent the morning and most of the afternoon with Laihar, the building's botanist I told you about, remember?"

"Right."

She did mention on their last date that she had met the man who'd designed the indoor gardens of the Liaison Committee building. He now supervised the army of drones and the AI that maintained the complex system of the indoor plants in every room there.

She never said, however, that she was on a first-name basis with him already.

"Laihar allowed me to shadow him for the day. It was a great way to gain insight into how all these gorgeous flowers are planted and maintained here in Voran."

Plants were her passion. Her face lit up when she talked about them. It pleased him that she enjoyed it so much. But the thought of someone else having her attention nearly the entire day caused a tendril of envy to slither into his chest.

"So, Laihar was good to you then?" He tapped his hoof on the soft rag covering his floor.

"Very good. He didn't leave my side, taking his time to explain everything to me and answering any questions I had."

"How so very nice of him," he muttered, wishing he could bury Laihar in one of his flowerpots. "Is he married?"

She gave him a curious look, the lipstick she was about to apply raised in her hand.

"No. He isn't. Never was apparently. He has four children, but they're all grown up now and no longer live with him."

She knew an awful lot about a man she'd just met. But they did spend the entire day together. They must've talked a lot.

"So, he's old then?" he asked with hope.

"Not really. He had children when he was young. So, I'd say he's in his early forties now. Still very fit and active."

"Is he now?" He winced.

Her eyes sparked with mischief.

"Laihar paints his horns in the colors of the flowers he works with that week. This week, he has purple stripes with yellow dots like the *umpheads* we planted."

"You like his horns?"

"I believe I do." She hiked a shoulder. "He does have nice horns."

The wisp of jealousy in his chest burned hotter.

Damned that botanist and his purple horns. *Purple*, Maya's favorite color...

Fuck.

"He also has a way with his tail," she continued. "He uses it to poke just the right size holes in the dirt to plant the *umpheads*."

Kear would love to show her all the things he wished to do to her with *his* tail if she just let him. Then, he'd use it to strangle that scoundrel botanist.

"So, you say his horns are longer than mine?"

She rolled her eyes. "I never said that. I didn't measure his horns. Or yours, for that matter. But I would like to work with this man again. So, chances are you'll meet him one day, and I won't appreciate you having some kind of horn-measuring contest with him. Okay?"

"He must like you."

Of course he did. Who in their own mind wouldn't like Maya? The sweet, beautiful, gentle Maya, whom Kear loved so much, he could hardly breathe.

"He says he does," she confirmed. "He offered to take me to the botanical exhibition tomorrow. It doesn't open for three days yet, but Laihar has early access passes—"

"Fuck!" He speared his fingers through the fur on his head, spinning on his hooves.

"Kear?"

He pivoted back to her.

"It's a date, Maya. He asked you out on a date. The asshole wants to date you."

"Laihar isn't an asshole," she reprimanded.

Oh yes, he is. He wants to take you away from me.

"But yes, he wants to date me," she admitted. "He was very clear on that."

Kear froze, chills spreading along his skin under his fur.

This was exactly the situation he'd been avoiding all his life. He'd witnessed the turmoil and heartache that his brothers had gone through. And now he was facing all of that himself.

Maya exhaled a laugh. "The guy didn't waste his time. He asked me out within the first hour we met."

That didn't surprise him. Women were rare in Voran. Single women, even more so. A man had to act fast if he wanted a chance at female attention.

"Relax, Kear." Maya shook her head, her expression shifting from playful to serious. "I told him I'm already seeing someone."

"That wouldn't stop a Voranian man from pursuing a woman," he replied bitterly.

Women in Voran often dated several men simultaneously and received multiple marriage proposals before choosing a husband. That was just a way of life on his planet, stemming from the severe population imbalance.

He never wished to join a dating game like this. But he wasn't going to retreat now. Maya was his, and he would fight for her, no matter how many rivals there were.

He had to come up with a plan. He'd known her the longest. He'd learned what made her smile and what she was passionate about. He knew the things she liked.

He'd take her to the most amazing places, on and off the planet. He'd break into that botanical exhibition as early as tonight if he had to. But he wasn't letting any other man have her, even if he happened to be a botanist with a career in the area that Maya loved.

"What we have won't stop Laihar from trying to win you from me," he said.

"Maybe." She finished applying the makeup and rose from her chair. "But *I* will. And I already did. I told him there could never be anything romantic between him and me. I'm already dating a man, and I don't want to date more than one."

He remained motionless, letting her words sink in and relief sweep through him.

"Kear," she spoke again, since he couldn't muster a word in reply yet. "I want to make it clear, I'm not choosing between men. I'm just trying to decide whether to stay with *you*. You are my one and only option. I don't need more. There is no competition."

He didn't deserve her.

She was way too good for him. But he would spend his entire life striving to be worthy of this woman. If only she let him be at her side for as long as they both should live.

"I'm coming over right now."

He'd sit on the floor by her door if he had to while she got ready. But he needed to be as close to her as was physically possible.

SHE DIDN'T MAKE HIM wait by the door. She let him in. By the time he arrived, her hair had been dried and styled into thick flirty waves. But she was still wearing nothing but the towel.

He grabbed her into a hug, needing to feel her.

"I love you." He nuzzled the side of her neck, breathing in her warm, fresh scent mixed with the soap aroma lingering after her shower.

She released a moan, melting into his touch.

"I love...hearing you say it."

These weren't exactly the words he yearned to hear from her. But she turned her face to his, eagerly catching his kiss on her lips.

He'd wait. He'd wait for as long as it took for her to say those words back to him.

She twined her arms around his neck, pressing her body to his. He ran his hands up her sides, feeling her every curve through the absorbent but thin towel.

His mind swam with lust. His cock throbbed so hard, he feared he would burst in his pants. She moaned when he cupped her breast through the sheet.

Then, she pulled away.

"I need to get dressed if we want to make it to the movie on time."

Fuck the movie. He wanted nothing more than to keep holding her just like this. But she'd already taken her hands off him.

He knew he deserved every prolonged moment of this torture. He endured it as an atonement for the way he'd wronged her before. He'd endure it for as long as it took for her to forgive him.

"The movie it is then," he conceded.

Chapter 28

Maya

The illuminated stage stood out against the receding evening light in the park. Actors played out a funny scene among the holographic backdrop and props.

This was my eleventh date with Kear in the past thirteen days. Even on the evenings when either his work in the lab or my job-shadowing with Laihar kept us apart, we still made time to talk before going to bed.

"I love this actress," I whispered to Kear as the audience laughed at a joke the female character made.

"Actor," Kear corrected, also keeping his voice down for the sake of other people in the audience. "This is an all-male theater group, like most groups in Voran. Men play all female roles."

The shortage of women affected all areas of life in Voran, but society had long learned to adapt.

"He's very talented."

"He is."

Anika squirmed, waking up in her bassinet next to me. It was a weekend, and Kear and I had picked her up from the academy that morning.

It still amazed me that a newborn would be in an academy. But that was the Voranian way of life. Babies had aptitude tests the day they were born, which determined the best areas for their development. Like her dad, scans of Anika's little brain showed a high potential for logic and analysis. She'd be raised as a scientist with an option to choose the area of her studies as she gets older.

Kear reached for his daughter, but I beat him to it.

"I've got her." I took the baby out and cuddled her against my chest.

By the second date with her father, I gave up trying to stay away from her. Regardless of how things went between Kear and me, I couldn't fight my fierce affection for the baby. I figured I could always love her, no matter how I felt about her father.

"Shhh, my sweet baby." I nuzzled the soft fur on her head. Pearly gray, it would turn darker as she grew older. I wished to be a part of her life as it happened, witnessing all her firsts, from her first word, to her first step, to her first academic achievement of which, I was sure, she would have many.

The fresh night breeze brushed by my arms, sending a light shiver down my body.

"Come here." Kear wrapped an arm around my shoulders.

He pulled me into his warmth, shielding me from the evening chill. I relaxed against his strong body. The baby calmed in my arms, tucked comfortably between us.

There was no better place I could imagine for myself. Not now, not ever.

"I'LL FLY YOU HOME," Kear said as the show ended and we walked toward a parking platform.

"You don't have to."

Taxi service was excellent in Voran.

"But I want to."

"You'll see me again, first thing tomorrow morning." We had a day trip planned out of the city, with an early start.

An elevator took us up to the parking platform.

He paused at his aircraft. "I still would like to fly you home."

Home.

My temporary accommodation at the Liaison Committee building never felt like home.

"Please?" Placing his hands on my waist, he lowered his head until our foreheads touched.

It was hard to resist him like that. Still I tried. "You need to get some sleep. You'll have to pick me up early, and Anika will probably keep you up at night."

"Then come with me. Stay at my place tonight, so we can leave together first thing tomorrow morning." His voice was soft, his breathing shallow, like he was afraid to take a deep breath, waiting for my answer.

"It would make sense for me to sleep over, wouldn't it?"

"You in my place always makes perfect sense," he agreed. Cupping my face, he guided my mouth to his and sealed his words with a gentle kiss.

"I have my bag packed already. I could just send a delivery service to bring it over."

He kissed me again. "See how practical it is?"

"And you have lots of spare bedrooms in your apartment," I continued, thinking out loud.

"Lots," he echoed, kissing the side of my face.

"All right, then. I'll come with you."

He grinned, as if I'd just handed him a huge Christmas present. Taking my hand in the aircraft, he didn't let go all the way to the hospital.

Anika woke up the moment we arrived.

"Hungry? Again?" I smiled.

"Always hungry," Kear lamented. "It's amazing how much a little being like that can eat. But then again, she poops a lot too."

I laughed, helping him unload the baby things from the aircraft. This "little being" also required us to bring along a lot of luggage anywhere she went.

Taking Anika from her bassinet, Kear held her against his shoulder. It was only his third weekend with her, but he handled her with ever-increasing ease and confidence. I caught him rubbing the side of his face against the tiny buds of the baby's horns.

He was slowly transforming from simply a biological father to a dad. And it was a wonderful transformation to witness.

"Shhh." He bounced on his hooves a little, calming Anika down. "Give me just a minute to get you some dinner." He grabbed the fake boob out of the bassinet and squeezed it to test for contents. "It looks like we're out, baby girl. You finished it all."

Holding the baby at his shoulder, he marched through the living room toward the kitchen, then stopped in his tracks as if remembering something.

"I need to go down to the lab to get more milk," he said, turning to me. "She ate all I had on hand. Must be going through a growth spurt."

My breasts tingled with build-up pressure. It was time for me to pump.

"I'll be quick." He started for the door.

"Wait." I stopped him. "She needs to eat. I need to pump. We could just, you know...bypass the pump and make it easier for everyone."

He paused, keeping his eyes on mine.

"You want to nurse Anika?"

"It'd be easier," I repeated, trying to sound casual, though I realized this was not a casual matter.

Judging by the look on his face, he knew it, too.

"Maya," he said carefully. "Breastfeeding facilitates bonding in humans. Leaving her would be that much harder for you, much harder than just leaving me."

Parting from either of them seemed impossible already.

I shook my head, reaching for the baby. "Just give her to me, Kear."

He didn't object anymore, handing Anika to me.

"Aww, come here, little princess," I cooed, making my way over to the couch.

Anika squirmed and wailed, her little button nose turning pink under the short fur.

"Hungry?" I smiled. "I know how it feels. I get cranky, too."

I sat down on the couch, adjusting her in the crook of my left arm. My dress closed on the back. The line where the two halves fused together ran from my neck down to my waist along my spine.

"Would you mind opening my dress for me, please?" I asked Kear, tilting down my head.

He grunted softly but stomped closer. I leaned forward, giving him more access. He reached over the high back of the couch and slid his fingers down, releasing the closure. His light touch skittered across my shoulders as he pushed the dress off my left side, taking the bra strap down with it.

Holding the baby on my arm, I freed my left breast. Anika turned her head, searching for the nipple. The moment I moved it closer, she latched onto it firmly. The fussing and crying stopped immediately. After a few impatient, hungry pulls, she found her rhythm, tugging gently as she nursed.

Her face relaxed. Her eyelids, trimmed with thick black eyelashes, fluttered open. She stared up at me with eyes of the same intense violet color as her dad's.

Tenderness swept through me. My limbs felt warm and heavy. I caught her hand, pressing my thumb in the middle of her little palm. I felt completely and utterly in love.

Kear brushed my hair out of the way and over my shoulder. Then I felt a press of his lips at the base of my neck from behind.

"Thank you," he whispered.

I didn't clarify what he was thanking me for. I simply reveled in this moment of the three of us together and enjoyed the happiness that curled inside me like a fluffy kitten.

After she finished nursing, Kear took Anika to bed. I got off the couch and straightened my clothes.

He jogged down the stairs just a few moments later.

"Fast asleep." He grinned. "She had a busy day. Lots of fresh air. I may even get some sleep tonight, too."

"I can stay in her room and feed her when she wakes. That way, you'll get some rest, and I'll catch a nap in the aircraft on the way to the waterfalls tomorrow while you fly us there."

He stalked toward me from the stairs.

"You can't ever leave us, Maya. Not anymore, not ever." He gripped my shoulders, his eyes trapping mine. "I'll win you over, no matter how long it will take me. I'll go to Earth with you if I have to. I'll do anything."

The intensity in his voice made me sway in his arms. I slid a glance down his face, pausing on his mouth.

"All you have to do right now is kiss me," I breathed out.

He didn't wait for me to ask him twice. Taking my face in his large hands, he claimed my mouth with his.

I grabbed the belt of his pants, drawing him closer.

"I love you," he purred between kisses. "I love you so much, my flower."

I slid my hands up his chest, then sank my fingers into the fur above his neckline.

"Take this off." I tugged at his shirt. "It's about time I got to see you naked, Professor."

Breath caught in his throat, then rasped out with a low growl. He tore at the shirt, ripping it off over his head.

"Mmm," I moaned, burying my face in the thick fur on his chest.

His warm, spicy scent enveloped me. Thick and long on his chest, his fur tapered to a thin trail crossing his abdomen graced with hard squares of muscles. I followed the trail with my fingers all the way down to the belt of his pants.

"These will have to come off, too." I looked up, batting my eyelashes at him.

His heart pounded under my hand splayed on his chest. But he didn't make a move.

"Do you want me, Kear?"

"More than anything in the Universe. You have no idea, Maya. I've been dreaming about you—"

"In the sex pods?"

"No." He exhaled a bitter laugh. "I haven't been to the spa in ages."

"Why not?"

"All a pod can give me is a poor imitation of you. But I want the real thing."

His words gripped me, making me weak in the knees. I staggered, and he grabbed my waist, steadying me.

"Not to say that I didn't daydream about being with you. Constantly." He grinned. "In every hot detail. To the point that both my hands are sore now."

I burst with laughter, twirling a finger in his fur. "Well. We'll take it easy on your *hands* tonight, then."

He moved his arms around me. "This needs to go off, too. That would be only fair, don't you think?"

His fingers made the familiar tap-dance down my spine, opening my dress. I let him slide it off my shoulders.

"This, too," he murmured, tugging at the band of my bra. He fumbled with its closure, releasing a frustrated huff. "What a devious contraption."

"It's scientist-proofed," I teased, but then took pity on him and flicked it open. "Your IQ is clearly too high to master it."

"Smartass," he laughed, but the sound stuck in his throat the moment I slid the straps off my shoulders. "Fuck." He drew me to him with an arm around my middle.

His other hand hovered over my breast. Slowly, reverently, he final-ly cupped it, giving it a slight squeeze.

"I don't understand men's fascination with breasts," I said. "You just saw them being used for their intended purpose—feeding a baby."

"As with many great things, your breasts have more than one pur-pose. And right now, their main one is to drive me mad with desire."

He lifted me in his arms until my chest was at his face level.

"Gorgeous," he murmured, giving each breast a tender kiss.

I ran my hands through his fur, then stroked his long smooth horns. He sucked in a breath, pressing his face to my chest. He held a topless woman in his arms for the first time ever, I realized. For the first time, he was touched intimately by a living person rather than a ma-chine.

My heart melted. Suddenly, I wished to give him everything he de-sired. I wanted to make this night special for him.

Sliding down his body, I gave him a quick kiss on the lips. "Pants off, Professor."

He sucked in a breath, but didn't argue, promptly unfastening his waistband.

I slid a hand inside.

"Maya..." He staggered on his hooves.

Being with Kear was different from my experience before. I'd never taken the lead in sex with Walter, who had been the one and only sex partner I'd had until now. This was new, a little unsettling, and very ex-citing, like I was playing a role of someone who wasn't me. Slipping in-to a different personality for a while felt like playing dress-up.

"Oh my God, you're huge," I gasped, trying to wrap my fingers around the hard, throbbing length in his pants. "How will I even fit you inside me?"

He hissed, tipping his head back in pleasure.

"A female birth canal can accommodate a wide range of girths. It expands under certain circumstances..."

I smiled. He was being a typical nerdy professor now, giving me a lecture. But I didn't want to shut him up. Playing along felt like more fun.

Squeezing his hard cock in my hand, I murmured, "But how about a female *mouth*, Professor Thormus? What are your thoughts on how accommodating it could be?"

He stuttered to a stop, mid-sentence.

"A mouth?"

"Mhm." I smiled innocently, sliding down his body to my knees. "Should we do some tests?"

I tugged his pants down his hips, freeing his erection. It looked as massive as it felt, rising from the thick fur in his groin. Smooth, dark-gray skin stretched like silk over the relief of bulging veins. Short, velvety fur covered the taut sack at the base. I cupped it in my hand, playing with the two spheres inside.

Holding his length in my other hand, I twirled the tip of my tongue around the crown.

"Maya, I..." he gasped for air like a man drawing in the sea of pleasure. "I won't last long like this."

"Then don't. I want to see you come." I dragged my tongue along his hard length, then sucked as much of it as I could into my mouth. I couldn't fit much in, but I made up for it by lapping at him with enthusiasm.

He tasted amazing, warm and spicy with a hint of salt. His moans and thrusts spurred my own arousal. I squirmed on my knees, pressing my thighs together.

His tail wrapped tightly around my waist, bringing me closer. He rested both hands on the sides of my head, cradling it gently. His hips bucked. His chest vibrated with a growl.

"Let it go, Kear, darling," rushed through my head.

I wanted to see him undone. By me, not by a machine for once.

He shifted on his hooves with a tortured groan. His cock spasmed, releasing warm spurts into my mouth. I swallowed in big gulps, but I couldn't keep up. Some dripped out, running down from the corners of my mouth.

Kear panted when I finally let go of him. Air rushed out of his chest in huge, ragged breaths. He staggered to the couch behind me and dropped into the seat as if cut down at his knees.

"Come here," he croaked.

Flexing his tail, he brought me closer, then grabbed me with his arms and dragged me into his lap.

"Are you alright?" I cupped his cheek.

He rested his head on the back of the couch, closing his eyes.

"It's like... So intense, Maya. It feels like jumping off a cliff, expecting to plummet to my death. But instead, finding myself flying." He opened his eyes, meeting mine. "I want to do it to you now. I want to taste you, too."

He flipped me on my back and quickly did away with my panties, then parted my thighs.

I held my breath, my fingers gripping the soft leather of the couch. He'd seen me like this, open and exposed, many times before. But the expression on his face was new. His bright eyes shone with excitement. Darting his tongue out, he licked his lips, like a kid in a candy store.

It was as if he finally realized what he'd been missing all his life. And now he wished to try it all.

"Wait." I pulled my knees closer, trapping his head between them. "Are you sure that's what you want? Wouldn't it be too much for the first time? It is your first time, Kear."

He grinned. "Not if you count all the things I've already done to you in my imagination."

With his head trapped between my knees, he slipped his tongue out between his lips. Dark-red and impossibly long, it stretched all the way down to my core. The tapered tip flicked my clit. Desire zapped through me, making my inner muscles clench.

"God... Kear."

My knees fell apart, releasing him. He flashed me a cocky grin before diving in. His tongue swirled around my opening, as if testing the waters. With a strangled sound of pleasure, he slipped it deeper.

Raking my fingers through his fur, I found his horns and wrapped my hands around them, holding on for dear life as he took me for a ride.

The tip of his tongue stroked me from the inside. It brushed by a spot that sent a wave of pleasure through my lower belly. I arched my back with a moan. He glanced up at me with a smug look in his eyes.

This might be his first time, but he knew exactly what he was doing. Professor Thormus built his entire career on studying female bodies. He spent well over a year learning everything specifically about my body. He knew my biology better than I knew it myself, and now he was using every piece of that knowledge to drive me crazy with need.

I lifted my hips to his mouth to take full advantage of his wicked skills.

With the tip of his tongue dancing inside me, he folded it at the base, pressing the wider, thicker part of that magnificent organ of his to my clit. I bucked my hips under the onslaught of pleasure.

He held my thighs open with his hands, working me with his tongue only, inside and out.

I slid my hands up and down his horns, then gripped the very tips of them, pressing my core into his mouth. Pleasure rolled through me. The approaching orgasm teased with heat licking up my thighs. His tongue rubbed me from the outside as its tip flitted inside me. The dual stimulation rocked my body with bliss I'd never felt before.

The intense sensation crested and exploded through me with all-consuming pleasure. For a few fantastic moments, there was just Kear and me in the entire Universe; everything else fell apart.

He kissed up my body, slowly taking me down from the intense high he'd just sent me to.

"How are you so good at this?" I panted.

He smiled against my breast, his tongue flicking my nipple. "Long hours of practicing it step by step in my head. With my cock fisted in my hand."

"Your poor little cock," I teased.

"Little?" He arched an eyebrow.

"Giant," I corrected myself. "Massive. Ginormous. I can't wait to feel it inside me. Even if it splits me in two."

He growled under his breath. His dark pupils dilated, taking over the pretty violet of his irises.

That ginormous cock of his pressed against my thigh. He was impossibly hard again. My inner muscles clenched, missing his tongue already.

He shifted higher, placing a kiss on my lips. It was gentle and sweet, his taste and mine mingling together. Palming my breast, he massaged it gently, stroking the tip with his thumb.

I wiggled my hips, rubbing against his erection.

"I want your tongue," I begged, pulling back.

Where did this come from? I wasn't sure. I used to love gentle and sweet. I still did. I enjoyed Kear's tenderness. But the feral need for this man raged inside me, demanding more.

He kissed my lips once again. His tongue snaked into my mouth, twirling inside it as I hungrily kissed him back. The length of his tongue wrapped around mine, the tip reaching nearly all the way to the back of my throat. Still, it wasn't enough.

I reached down, running my hands along his hard, throbbing cock. He broke our kiss with a sharp exhale.

"Fuck me, Kear," I demanded. "Hard."

I should probably take him upstairs to his bedroom. Let him make love to me on his terms, in a proper bed. For all intents and purposes, he was still a virgin. I owed it to him to do it right.

Only everything we did already felt so right. More right than anything I'd ever had before.

"I never wanted anyone in my life as much as I want you," I moaned.

With a satisfied growl, Kear rose on his knees above me. Fisting his erection, he gave it one slow pump. His eyes remained on mine. He licked his lips as if ready to devour me.

Heat rushed through me from his attention. I felt no need to hide from his exploring gaze. I ran my hands up my sides, cupping my breasts and tugging on my nipples. Pleasure rippled along my skin, teasing with desire for more.

Sitting up, I gripped his hips.

"I want your ginormous dick inside me, Kear. Now."

With a deep, low grunt, he flipped me over, my face to the back of the couch. I arched my back, thrusting my ass out in his direction.

A knee placed on each side of me, he slid his cock between my thighs. I parted my legs a little wider, giving him more space.

He leaned over me, rasping in my ear, "You want me to fuck you? Hard and raw?"

God, it shouldn't feel as hot as it did, should it? My legs shook, desire clenching in my lower belly.

"Yes, please." I reached between my legs, guiding him inside me.

He was huge, but I felt hot and slick after the orgasm he'd given me. He eased in a little. I moved back against him, taking more of him in.

"Maya...sweetheart," he exhaled, dropping his head to my shoulder. "Fuck, you feel..."

"Better than a sex pod?" I giggled.

He moaned into my shoulder. "There is no comparison."

Holding my hips tight, he pulled out a little, only to slam back in again.

"Yesss," I hissed, gripping the back of the couch. "Just like that. All the way."

He was so thick and impossibly long. His invasion felt absolute, taking over my body and all my senses.

"Fuck me, Kear." I thrust back against him, pressing my forehead into the back of the couch.

Thrust after thrust, his control was slipping. He growled louder, moving faster, slamming inside me like a feral beast.

Lust raged in me, setting my blood on fire. I clawed at the leather of the couch, struggling to stay upright under the onslaught of his passion. His tail slipped around my right thigh, stroking the sensitive skin on the inside. The arrowhead tip brushed by my clit, sending a shot of heat through my body.

I whimpered in pleasure, burying my mouth into the back of the couch. He pressed his tail against my clit, rubbing harder. I bit into the leather as my climax neared. Wild, needy sounds tore from me. I rocked against Kear's cock like a woman possessed. The orgasm gripped me. Hot, mind-blinding ecstasy rolled through me. The release was so intense, I sank my teeth into the leather, growling with abandon.

Kear dropped on top of me. His large body curled over mine, both shuddering with climax.

My teeth left a deep mark in the back of the couch.

"Sorry, I ruined your furniture," I panted, coming down from the crest of passion and back into reality.

What had gotten into me? I'd acted insane. Walter would've been shocked and appalled if I bit and growled like that during sex with him. He'd probably have me committed to an institution or something.

Kear just laughed, catching his breath.

"I've done worse to this poor couch. I've accidentally stabbed it with my horns once or twice while fantasizing about all the things I'd do to you if I ever got you on it."

"Either way, it's all my fault, then? I should just replace this couch. With something far more durable. A metal bench maybe?"

He laughed again, gathering me into his arms.

"I love you, my flower. And I'll wait for as long as it takes for you to say these words back to me."

I caught a quick kiss from him on my lips.

"You don't have to wait, Kear. I fell in love with your letters. I fell so hard, it broke my heart to learn the man behind them wasn't real."

"But I am real." He pressed me closer to him. "I've never been more real than when I wrote those letters to you. And I will stay real and true to you, for as long as you choose to be with me."

There was no dissonance this time. The person behind the words that I fell in love with merged with the man holding me in his arms, forming one and only Kear.

"I love you," I said, feeling it with all my heart. "Ask me again how long I'm staying in Voran."

He paused, then swallowed hard before asking quietly, "How long are you staying, Maya?"

"Indefinitely." I met his eyes with a smile. "For as long as we both want. Or at least for as long as what we have feels right."

Air rushed out of him in a gush of relief. He sat on the couch, cradling me in his lap.

"Sweetheart." He kissed my hair. "I promise to make it feel right forever. And if at any time something feels wrong to you, please talk to me and I'll do everything to right it all again."

Epilogue

Kear

One year later

Anika giggled, running down the beach to the water, her tiny hooves leaving neat round dents in the luscious grass of the riverbank.

"Get back here, you little rascal!" Maya dashed after their daughter.

The baby tripped, still unsteady on her hooves since she'd been walking for just over a month now. She tumbled down the bank and splashed into the water.

Kear held his breath, even as he knew the river was shallow along the bank here. He trusted Maya could handle this. But his protective instincts made him stand to attention, ready to jump in if needed.

Anika's purple bathing suit inflated on contact with the water, and she floated, splashing with her hands and giggling with glee.

"Where do you think you're swimming to, missy?" Holding her long wrap skirt up, Maya waded into the water and fished the baby out.

Anika kicked her hooves, squealing in protest.

"I'll take her," he offered, opening his arms.

"You want to go to Daddy?" Maya asked.

"Dada!" Anika reached for him with her arms and her tail.

Among the usual baby gibberish, that one word had been more and more prominent in her vocabulary. Every time it slipped from his daughter's chatty mouth, a warm wave of pride rolled over him.

"That's right," Maya cooed, blowing a raspberry on one of Anika's chubby cheeks. "Dada is here." She sighed. "Can you say Mama, now?"

"Dada!" the baby giggled as he took her.

"Well, maybe later."

The Voranian word for "dad" was short and easy to pronounce for babies. Though Maya insisted that "mama" was also easy to say in her language. Unlike most babies in Voran, Anika didn't have the translator implant yet. He and Maya decided to wait with it so that she could learn to speak both languages of her parents first.

Barely avoiding getting kicked by the tiny hooves, Kear carried the baby to the portable shallow pool he had specifically put on the riverbank for Anika to splash in safely.

"That's as far as you can swim for now, cutie pie." He put the baby in the pool that had brightly colored toys mounted along the edges. A few floating ones splashed in the water, less than two hands' lengths from the bottom.

The baby plopped down on her bum, her bathing suit keeping her afloat. She reached for a toy, while sticking another one into her mouth. Hopefully, the pool would occupy her long enough for him and Maya to eat lunch.

While Maya arranged the trays with food on the blanket spread over the grass, he opened two small containers of flavored water.

After they ate, Maya changed Anika and nursed her on the blanket while he cleaned up after lunch, furtively watching his wife and baby. Nursing seemed to completely absorb them both, making them look lost in each other.

He loved watching Maya's face. It glowed with serenity. A peaceful smile played on her lips as she gently stroked Anika's chubby cheek with a finger. The baby's eyelids dropped, heavy with exhaustion after a busy morning.

His two favorite women. They often threw his carefully organized routine into disarray. But he wouldn't have it any other way.

There were no more secrets between his wife and him. He'd told her all about Walter's letter that he'd stopped from reaching her long ago and about that Rhea woman her ex was seeing. Apparently, Walter had contacted Maya's mother a few months ago, looking for Maya to convince her to invest in his sporting goods store that wasn't doing well. Maya quickly put a stop to that, forbidding that piece of shit from bothering her or any of her loved ones ever again.

They had never heard from him since. Hopefully, they never would.

Maya finished feeding the baby and carefully placed her into the bassinet. Lowering the sun canopy over the bassinet, she turned on the sleep monitoring system that would alarm them when Anika woke up or if the baby was in distress.

"Ahhh." His wife stretched her back and shoulders, running her gaze over the river with the wide waterfall on the opposite bank. "It's so gorgeous here. I'll never get used to it or take it for granted."

The property had been in Kear's family for four generations. He remembered coming here as a child with his grandfather. The cabin up the riverbank was small but neat, with all the amenities necessary to have a relaxing family trip away from the city.

"Has your father left Voran City yet?" Maya asked, sauntering to the blanket on the ground where he sat stretching his legs.

The sun streaked her black tresses with gloss and put a spark in her eyes. The cropped top of her bathing suit gently cradled her breasts, allowing them to bounce gently with every step. The wide, air-thin shawl she had tied around her curvy hips like a wrap skirt billowed in the breeze.

His wife was and always would be the most beautiful woman in the Universe to him.

"When is your dad getting here?" she asked again.

"Just before dinner. He sent me a message this morning that he still wanted to stop by the Earth Girl's Desserts."

Her face split with a wide smile. "He's bringing cupcakes?"

His wife had a sweet tooth, and from the moment his father had learned about that, he'd never failed to indulge her.

"He sure loves spoiling you." Kear heaved an exaggerated sigh.

"And I love him for it." She kept grinning.

Her family was planning to visit them one day soon. But Maya fit in perfectly with his family, too. His father doted on her and Anika. His brothers adored them both. It couldn't be any other way. Sweet and gentle with everyone, Maya was so easy to love. And Anika just happened to be the most adorable baby in the world, in his opinion.

Along with his father and his brothers, they expected quite a few more guests for dinner tonight. They'd come from the city for a visit and some would stay overnight in the portable shelters they were bringing with them.

A few months ago, Voran had officially acknowledged tomorrow's date as the national day to celebrate all fathers. It happened with a significant push from the group of Earth women married to Voranian men.

Fathers in Voran had been largely responsible for raising Voranian children. Most did it on their own, humbly not expecting recognition. It never even occurred to Kear before that celebrating parenthood could be done on a national level.

Now, however, he was looking forward to getting together with his extended family. Still very much a loner outside of his work and family, Kear didn't have many friends. But Maya insisted on inviting some of his colleagues and patients whose children he had helped to bring into the world.

In a couple of hours, it'd be busy here. The noise of music, conversations, and children's laughter would break the usual lazy calm around the river. But for now, it was still just their little family here. And with the baby peacefully asleep, he had Maya all to himself.

"Come to me," he murmured, sliding his wife onto his lap.

He'd learned many romantic phrases by now and had composed even more of them himself. But "come to me" was one of the most meaningful and the most underrated ones, in his opinion.

"Come to me, and I'll make it all better."

"Come to me, I'll give you comfort."

"Come to me, life is perfect when you're near."

"Come to me, I need you…"

He nuzzled her cheek, sliding his hand inside her top.

"Kear," she gasped. "We'll have guests coming soon."

"Not for the next two hours, at least." He kissed her lips, tugging on the bottom one with his teeth.

"Well. As you wish, Professor." A teasing note rang in her voice. Her eyes were hooded in a seductive expression that sent a spear of heat through his groin.

He loved his wife deeply with all his heart. But her playful moods brought his love to all new heights.

She shifted in his lap to face him while straddling his thighs.

"I've been suffering from something I hope you can help me with, Professor Thormus." She batted her eyelashes.

His heart thudded in anticipation as his cock sprang to attention.

"Symptoms?" His voice came out raspy from lust.

He withdrew his hands from her body and balled them into fists. She wished to play the role of his patient. And it wouldn't do to fondle a patient, no matter how badly he wished to ravage this particular one.

"It aches. Right here." She lifted her hips off his thighs and slid a hand under her shawl-skirt.

He followed her gesture with his eyes, swallowing hard.

"Also, my chest tingles. Right here." She slid her other hand into the neckline of her top.

He could see through the fabric that she tugged at her nipple, making it pebble. Her other nipple hardened too, poking against the thin material of her top.

His mouth watered. He swallowed again, licking his lips. Her attention immediately snapped to his tongue. He knew she enjoyed it when he used it on her. He opened his mouth wider, curving his tongue to slide the tip over his teeth. She squirmed in his lap with a soft whimper.

"Sounds serious." He'd tried to maintain a professional tone, but a growl slipped in, tickling his throat with vibration.

"It does?" She made big eyes in fake horror. "Can you help me, Professor?"

"Let's see what I can do. Take off your top, please."

She pouted, hiding a smile.

"Do I have to?"

"I need to examine you, Madam Maya. Show me exactly where it aches, tingles, and throbs."

"I didn't say anything about throbbing. I don't have that particular symptom."

"Oh, you will," he promised to a flash of delight in her eyes. "I'll make sure you will. And very soon, too." He folded his arms across his chest, leaning back. "Now do as I say and remove your top."

Dropping her gaze, she lifted a shoulder, sliding the wide strap off it.

He held his breath as the fabric of her top slid lower, revealing more of her smooth brown skin. The dusky arch of her areola came into view. Then the hard bud of the nipple popped out.

"Do you need to see this one, too?" she asked innocently, cupping her other breast through her top.

"Both…" he rasped, watching her squeeze her breast and play with the tip. "Both, please."

Torturously slow, she tugged the other strap down too, flicking her nipple with the edge of the neckline on its way.

"What do you think?" With her hands under her breasts, she lifted them both up, as if presenting them to him.

"Fantastic. They're just fantastic," he muttered, forgetting all about the game and his role in it. "So hot and delicious."

"Don't you need to examine them, Professor?"

"Right. Of course." He lifted his hands. "I'll be touching your breasts now, Madam Maya. Please describe exactly what you feel when I'm doing it."

He cupped both mounds with his hands. Much larger than hers, his hands fit around each breast perfectly. He massaged them, gently squeezing the nipples between his fingers.

She gasped, rubbing her core against his thigh.

"It feels good, Professor. So, so good."

He kept his voice steady and impassive, despite the lust raging through his body. "More tingling or less?"

"More..." She moaned, arching her back. "Definitely more."

"Good." He flicked his tongue out, wrapping the tip around her erect nipple.

She tilted her head down, watching his tongue squeeze and tug.

"What are you doing, Professor?"

He retrieved his tongue.

"Taste test," he explained. "A regular part of an examination."

With his arm around her middle, he drew her closer, then sucked the entire tip of her breast into his mouth. She gripped the fur on the back of his head. The tug of her fingers sent ripples of arousal down his chest and to his groin.

She shifted closer, sliding along the hard ridge of his erection. He swallowed a groan, rolling the bud of her nipple between his teeth.

"Does the taste test need to be done on all my parts that ache and throb?" she asked.

"So, there *is* throbbing present, now?" he enquired in his best professional tone of voice, though it was nearly impossible to maintain it with her tit in his mouth.

"Oh, it is present, Professor. Just as you said it would be."

"Show me where?" He curled his tail around her leg, snaking it higher up her thigh. "Here, by any chance?" He wormed the tip of his tail between her legs.

She cursed under her breath, bucking her hips when he brushed by her pleasure spot.

He clicked his tongue disapprovingly, even as his desire spiked, "What a filthy mouth you have on you, Madam Maya. It's unfortunate we can't use spanking as a corrective method of your behavior."

Neither of them was into the kind of play that involved spanking. But he knew Maya loved the stern tone of his reprimands.

"I'll do better, Professor. Please, please find out what's wrong with me. I *need* to have this throbbing stop."

"I'm afraid it will get much worse before it gets any better," he warned, untying the shawl from around her hips. "But there are a few things we can try. Do you trust me to make it better?"

"I do," she replied with no hesitation.

Taking her in his arms, he laid her down with her back to the blanket, then eased her tight swim shorts down her legs.

"Open wider for me, Maya," he said softly. And she obediently parted her knees, exposing herself to him.

He didn't need to touch her to see how wet she was. The delicate lips of her sex glistened with her arousal.

"You have the most gorgeous puss... um, *reproductive organ* I've ever seen."

"It means a lot coming from you," she quipped. "You have seen quite a few."

A smile tugged at the corners of his mouth, making it hard to stay in the role.

"What are you going to do to me, Professor?" Maya's deliberately timid question brought him back on track.

"First, I will find the epicenter of your suffering." Holding her knees open with his hands, he drew circles on her inner thigh with his tail, moving it closer and closer to her core.

Her chest moved with shallow breathing. Her breasts heaved enticingly. He leaned forward, taking them in his hands again.

Maya arched an eyebrow. "I thought we were done with *their* examination."

"It's good to keep them, um...warm," he made up the lamest explanation. His brain was too clouded with need to come up with anything better.

"Is that what you're doing?" Maya narrowed her eyes at him. "Keeping them warm?"

"And moist." He dragged his tongue over a nipple, then nibbled at it with his lips.

That stopped her from questioning him. Her eyelids dropped in pleasure. She arched her back, pressing her breast into his mouth.

He flicked his tail over her hot, swollen clit.

"Oh God..." she gasped, raising her butt off the ground in search of more.

She was so ready for him. All it'd take would be just a few more tugs and strokes to make her come. But it was too much fun to play, and he tried to prolong it as much as they both could possibly stand.

He admired the sight of her, spread out in front of him, her skin flushed, her long hair spread around her head like flower petals. Her eyes closed, she was lost to the sensations taking over her body.

Dragging his tail between her slick, heated folds again, he enjoyed the sight of her trembling thighs. Muscles under her skin rippled. She flexed her fingers, clutching the blanket in her fingers.

"I need your cock," she groaned, lost to all-consuming need.

"That is a rather peculiar request, Madam Maya," he chuckled.

She reached between them, squeezing his erection through his beach shorts.

"Get this thing inside me, *Professor*. And fuck me. Hard."

Lust rocked him. Hot and demanding. Shoving his swim shorts down, he rose over her on his knees. Grabbing her hips, he flipped her over onto her belly, then lifted her butt and aligned his length with her opening.

"You want it hard, Maya?"

She released a needy whimper in reply, thrusting her hips back against him. He slammed inside her, meeting her thrust. She groaned, speared with his cock. He tugged her closer to him, dragging the blanket she clutched in her fists.

"God...you're huge," she moaned. "So, so good."

Her inner muscles gripped him tightly. Heat licked up his thighs. The climax wasn't far away now. It never was far when he was buried inside his wife's...*birth channel,* like this.

He thrust harder. Her heavy breasts swayed under her. She whimpered in pleasure every time her nipples dragged along the blanket. He leaned over her, grabbing her breasts in his hands to play with the tips.

Using his tail, he found her clit again without looking. She bucked under him as he stroked it.

"Harder..." she panted. "Please, Kear..."

He was "professor" only up to a certain point in their foreplay. "Kear" was always the one who fucked her. Because now, it was raw and real between them, leaving no room for games.

He could no longer deny her anything. He slammed into her harder, just as she wished. She rocked her ass against him, arching her back under the relentless caress of his tail.

"Come, Maya," he gritted through his teeth, his cock throbbing and ready to explode.

She groaned wildly and stilled. Her inner muscles spasmed around him. Her legs trembled. She moaned through her orgasm. And he let go, too, meeting her in pleasure.

She slackened, her shoulders rising and falling with her rapid breaths. He gathered her into his arms. Kissing the back of her neck, he lowered them both to the blanket.

"Feeling better, Madam Maya?"

"Much better, Professor." She grinned, turning in his arms to face him. "They don't lie when they call you a genius. A medical miracle."

He drew her in for a kiss. "Miracles happen when I'm with you."

She glanced up the river bank to the baby's bassinet placed under a tree.

"We're so lucky our baby is such a good sleeper."

"During the day, at least." He smirked.

Anika still was up once or twice at night, leaving them both exhausted in the morning. But at least she was the best at naps.

He ran his hands up and down his wife's back, enjoying the smooth glide of her skin under his palms. He cupped her bottom, getting a good handful. She shifted closer, wedging a leg between his thighs. He wound his tail around her ankle, his cock rising again.

"I'm afraid we'll need to repeat the treatment." He smiled against her skin, kissing her shoulder. "Just to be sure."

"Well, if we must..." She wiggled her butt, his cock rubbing against her inner thigh.

Blood rushed to his groin anew. Anticipation buzzed through his body, eager for him to take his wife again and again.

This was his first Father's Day, and it already was the best Father's Day in his life.

Married to Krampus

Chapter 1

"Daisy! How're you doing, my baby sister?" The image of Lily's face filled the screen of the ship's communication device I'd gotten permission to use.

"Um... I'm great, actually." I rolled my shoulders back and stretched my neck.

Physically, my muscles still ached and cramped a bit after the five-months long stasis sleep. Thankfully, my journey was almost over. I'd woken up yesterday and only had one more day to spend on this spaceship that was taking me to the country Voran on the planet Neron, the home world of my potential future husband.

Emotionally, I felt even better. Expectant. Elated. Happy, even. Maybe that was the aftereffect of all the drugs and vaccinations I'd received in the past several hours since waking up, but it felt so good to be awake.

"I'm great, Lily." I flicked a strand of my hair back over my shoulder, noting how limp and dull it had become. I should wash and curl my hair before landing tomorrow.

My heart leaped with excitement at the thought of finally meeting Colonel Grevar Velna Kyradus, the man with whom I might spend the rest of my life. Goosebumps rushed down my arms at the thought.

"Are you ready for the landing?" Lily asked.

"So ready! Honestly, I can't wait." I even bounced on the chair a little. Waiting for tomorrow felt very much like Christmas Eve, my favorite time of the year.

I drew in a long breath, calming myself. "How are you doing, Lily? How is everyone?"

"Oh, the usual." She waved me off, swiping a strand of her hair away from her face. Medium reddish-blonde, her hair color was the same as mine. Unlike my long and still matted from sleep locks, however, Lily's was neatly cut and styled into an impeccable bob. "Max and I are working. Kids are in school. Mom and Dad have just left for vacation... But please tell me more about the flight. You're the farthest anyone in our family has ever been, sister."

Actually, I was the farthest *most* people from Earth had been. The first contact with the Voranians from the planet Neron had happened barely a decade ago. There'd been a few visits by political delegations and scientific missions between our planets, but I was the very first regular person traveling that way.

"Five months is a long time to travel," Lily went on.

"Well, I slept through most of it." I laughed.

I'd had the choice to stay awake during the trip. The seven members of the Earth-Neron Liaison Committee, who were traveling with me, remained awake, but they had work to do. I'd just be wandering around the ship for the entire five months, anxious with anticipation for my arrival. I now had less than a day to wait, and I already felt wracked with nerves and excitement.

"We're all so proud of you, Daisy," Lily gushed.

My cheeks warmed with pleasure at hearing that. Normally, Lily had been the pride of the family, and rightfully so. My older sister had gone to college, got a well-paying office job upon graduation, married an amazing guy, and had the two sweetest children.

After a quarter of a century in this world, I hadn't achieved any of that. The bakery where I'd started working straight out of high school closed when its owner, Ms. Goodfellow, retired. I'd moved back in with my parents and worked odd babysitting jobs ever since.

I loved working with children. They had the uncanny ability to make a person forget about their troubles. However, the fact that I had no career, no partner in life, and no place in the world to call my own had been harder to deal with the older I got.

When the application for the Liaison Program had been made public, I applied on a whim. The opportunity to travel to another planet, live among an alien race, and learn a new culture enticed me. Without a boyfriend, a job, or even an apartment, I didn't have much to give up. The position on the application was stated as "Potential Spouse." And frankly, the prospect of an out-of-this-world romance appealed to me, too.

Never in a million years had I thought I'd be the one chosen out of the thousands of applicants. I'd expected a long selection process with several rounds, but the reply came a week after the application submission deadline.

When I saw my name as the selected candidate, it felt like I'd finally achieved something.

"Has he called you yet?" Lily asked.

My smile slipped off.

Colonel Kyradus, my "Potential Spouse," hadn't contacted me at all. There'd been no messages, no calls, no communication, nothing.

I snapped my spine straight and plastered the smile back on my face.

"The Colonel is meeting me upon landing, and I'll be there in less than twenty-four hours, so..."

"Hmm." Lily pursed her lips. "It's rather weird, don't you think, Daisy? Wouldn't a man be eager to talk to his bride? He hasn't even seen you, other than the application picture."

"Well, it's not a typical situation. I'm hardly his bride..."

I wasn't thinking about myself as a bride or a wife yet, though the papers I'd signed were titled, "Marriage Contract."

Voranians' birth rate had historically been hovering at about one girl to ten boys. In ancient times, their families comprised a wife with multiple husbands. Since all the technological advancements and cultural developments had taken place, the Voranian society had eventually moved on to a single partner marriage. Now, a wife only had one husband.

With women being so few, most men never got married. However, every healthy male could have a family on his own. Artificially inseminated, the married females carried the babies of the unmarried males.

Multiple births were a norm. As a result, the Voranians didn't have repopulation problems. Having reached a healthy birth rate in their country, they even ensured the slight population growth required to support their economy.

They weren't interested in human females as breeders. Scientists had determined humans and Voranians weren't genetically compatible to reproduce, anyway. Though, physiologically, the two species could have sex.

Since Voran ended up being populated predominantly by single dads, the role of a human woman would be that of a companion as well as a child caregiver, I imagined.

And that made my heart melt.

The Colonel had two young boys, five-year-old twins, and I was dying to meet them. I had yet to see any images of them.

When I woke up, I'd hoped some kind of communication would have come from the Colonel during my five months of sleep. There had been nothing, and I couldn't help being disappointed.

I hid it from Lily now, smiling wider than ever. There was no need to upset my sister.

"I'll get to meet his entire family soon enough."

Her frown of concern didn't ease.

"I hope Voranians look better in person," she sighed.

"Lily!" I threw my hands up in the air. "You can't hold their appearance against them. For all we know, they're lovely people."

"I know, I know… They're just so scary-looking."

We'd all seen the footage of the official meetings of Voranians with our politicians, and the videos of scientific expeditions to Neron. In addition, I had a photograph of Colonel Kyradus. It was a head shot of him I'd received along with the confirmation letter from the Liaison Committee.

The Colonel was definitely not someone a human would call beautiful. Or handsome. Or even pleasant to look at. In addition to the typical Voranian long horns and scruffy, charcoal fur, his blood-red eyes were, well… "scary-looking." Terrifying, actually.

The moment I first saw his picture, my breath stuck in my throat, and my heart dropped into my stomach. I hid the picture in a kitchen drawer for a while, afraid to keep it in my room or to look at it, especially at night.

Over the course of the few weeks it took me to get ready to leave Earth, however, I'd gotten used to the picture, and even had it as the background photo on my cellphone.

The Colonel's looks meant nothing, I'd decided. Behind terrifying appearances could live the most amazing personalities. Just like many handsome men were major douche bags once you got to know them better. I should know, I'd had my share of pretty boyfriends who'd turned out to be real assholes.

Though, I would've liked to get more pictures or videos of him and his family, the image of the Colonel's flaming red eyes in the picture no longer terrified me.

I'd read and watched everything I could get my hands on about Neron, Voranians, and their culture. Unfortunately, it wasn't much. They had provided me with general information, but I wanted something more personal to give me an idea of the man, his family, and his home that might all become mine, too, one day.

"Lily, I honestly don't care about his looks. I'm sure the Colonel is a nice person, and we'll get alone wonderfully," I said, voicing my wish out loud.

"Daisy, he would have to be a real asshole to *not* get along with you," Lily said in her usual big-sister, no-nonsense tone. "You're a sweetheart, honey. Everyone loves you."

A warm feeling spread through my chest. This was the reassurance I needed. Everything would be fine. Things could always be worked out between people, even if they came from two different planets.

"Aww, Lily. Thank you." I placed my hand next to her face on the screen, missing her and the rest of my family, now. "I love you so much."

"I love you, too, sweetie. And don't worry," she added hurriedly. "You'll do great. You're super easy to get along with. I'll be waiting for your messages, though."

I'd been told I would be able to send written messages to my family on a weekly basis and could have video communication with them on special occasions.

"I'll write every week," I promised.

Lily paused for a moment. Her desire to keep it positive was clearly warring with the big sister's need to warn and protect.

"If anything goes wrong or something doesn't work out..." she started.

"It'll be fine," I assured her. "In the worst-case scenario, I'd just come back to Earth in a year. Either way, it'll be an adventure."

As excited as I'd been to receive the confirmation letter, I had made sure to read the Marriage Contract very carefully before signing it. There was a condition that stated both parties had the right to dissolve the agreement for any reason, after the first full year of the union.

The way I viewed it, this was a year-long employment opportunity on another planet, with an added possibility for romance, which made it that much more exciting.

"Oh, I almost forgot, Daisy." Lily suddenly appeared uncharacteristically flustered. "There is this video that came to your email account here just after you've left. I asked the Committee to forward it to you. It's from the Colonel…"

"A video? From the Colonel?" A new wave of excitement flushed over me. He did send me something, after all. I'd just missed it by having boarded the spaceship already.

"Yes. I can't believe I almost forgot, but it's been five months now, and it slipped my mind… I'm so sorry."

"It's alright." I waved off her apologies. "I can watch it right now, then."

"Yeah, well." She bit her lip again. "Good luck, Daisy. Be careful, okay? And get out of there as soon as you can if anything goes wrong…"

We said our goodbyes, and I tried not to dwell too much on the reasons behind the worry on my sister's face. Instead, I allowed the excitement from finally getting a video to take over.

I quickly logged onto the ship's internal system and found the folder with my name. It contained all the information I had collected on Voran so far. The forwarded video file was also there.

The video took a few moments to load, and I got up from my seat in the ship's communication room to stretch my legs. Glancing at the progress bar from time to time, I paced the small room.

The ship was enormous, with a private cabin for me. My bed proved comfortable enough, but I was looking forward to feeling the ground of a planet under my feet, soon.

I wished I knew more about my destination, too. Waiting for the video to load, I wondered what would be in it.

I hoped this would be the Colonel's home video. The twins' birthday celebration, maybe? Or a family trip? Maybe a dinner with the Colonel and the boys. I would love to see a holiday celebration.

My favorite holiday had always been Christmas. Grandma and I used to bake and decorate early when she'd been alive. I even brought her favorite ornament to Neron with me. Since I would celebrate Christmas away from home this year, I wanted to have something with me that would remind me of my family and of Grandma.

A dinging sound announced the loading of the video was complete, and I rushed back to the screen.

It would be nice to see the Colonel in a casual setting. The one and only picture I had was of him in the dress uniform of the Voranian Army. In it, he was staring straight into the camera. Maybe that was what made his eyes look so exceptionally red? No one turned out good in official photos, right? I had my share of awkward pictures and often used pretty filters when posting photos of myself on social media.

The video opened.

Within seconds, I realized this was not a family celebration. The first image that came up was that of a metal wall. Then, a screeching sound hurt my ears. The wall split open, letting in a bright gush of light.

The landscape of an unknown planet filled the screen—bright red sand and unfamiliar, lush green vegetation.

The camera must have been mounted on someone's body, as the image was unsteady and accompanied by the heavy breathing of the person wearing it. As they turned, a Voranian military aircraft came into view. It appeared to have suffered an accident. It was lying on its side, its shiny metal hull crushed and dented.

A group of what I had first thought were gray boulders on the red ground started moving toward the person with the camera. As they came closer, it became apparent the things were alive.

Approaching the camera, they didn't slow down, menacingly moving closer. Several thin protrusions extended from their large, lumpy bodies. The closest blob of flesh lunged forward, knocking the camera off. It fell to the ground, the image breaking into stripes and dots before disappearing completely.

The next moment, the video resumed from a different angle—a camera from the damaged ship must have turned on. The group of gray blobs attacked a huge Voranian male who looked almost small in comparison.

Bare from the waist up, the Voranian fought fiercely. His fur, slick with sweat and blood, plastered against his bulging muscles as he punched the gray blobs of flesh with his fists and tore at them with his horns.

With a deep growl, he sank his fingers, tipped with long black claws, into one of the blobs attacking him. Baring his teeth in a terrifying grimace, he ripped the flesh apart, drenching himself in the pulsing gush of his enemy's blood.

The camera zoomed in on his face as he tilted his head back and released a deafening roar. The close-up of the Colonel's red eyes left no doubt that it was indeed my "potential spouse" out there, ripping living things to pieces with his bare hands.

Paralyzed by shock, I stared at the screen long after the video had ended.

Was this the man I had to live with? Was that how he behaved at home, too? A shudder ran through me. Was a loving marriage possible with someone like that? Could I even spend a year in his employment?

His poor children...

"Daisy. Are you okay?" A touch to my shoulder brought me out of my troubled thoughts. Nancy, one of the Earth's representatives to the Liaison Committee, gazed at me with concern.

Absorbed by the horrors playing out in the video, I hadn't noticed when she'd entered the room.

"I'm fine..." I mumbled, the nightmarish image of the Colonel's brutal expression frozen in my mind. "I'll be fine... Won't I?"

Available now.

More by Marina Simcoe

My Holiday Tails
Married to Krampus
My Tiny Giant
My Birthday Getaway
New Year, New Planet
Mail Order Mom
My Pumpkin
What Makes an Alien a Dad?

Dark Anomaly Trilogy
Gravity
Power
Explosion

Standalone Novels
Experiment
Enduring

The World of the River of Mists

Call of Water
Madness of the Moon
Power of Rage

Call of Water
Madness of the Moon
Power of Rage

Paranormal Romance

<u>*Demons (Complete Series)*</u>
Demon Mine
The Forgotten
Grand Master
The Last Unforgiven - Cursed
The Last Unforgiven - Freed

<u>*Stand Alone Novels Set in Demons World*</u>
The Real Thing
To Love A Monster

<u>*Midnight Coven Author Group*</u>
Wicked Warlock (Cursed Coven)

About the Author

Marina Simcoe likes to write love stories with characters, who may or may not be entirely human, because she firmly believes that our contemporary world could always use a little bit of the extraordinary.

She has lots of fun exploring how her out-of-this-world characters with their own beliefs, values, and aspirations fit into our every-day life.

She lives in Canada with her very own family man, their three little kids, and a cat, who is definitely out of this world.

For updates on her future books please visit Marina Simcoe Author page on Facebook or www.marinasimcoe.com.

Please Stay in Touch

If you enjoy my work, please consider joining my Patreon for early access to my WIP, custom art, ebooks, and signed paperbacks:

Newsletter signup is on www.marinasimcoe.com
Facebook Readers' Group:
Marina's Reading Cave
www.instagram.com/marinasimcoeauthor
www.marinasimcoe.com
www.facebook.com/MarinaSimcoeAuthor/
www.amazon.com/author/marinasimcoe
www.bookbub.com/profile/marina-simcoe
www.goodreads.com/MarinaSimcoe

www.ingramcontent.com/pod-product-compliance
Lightning Source LLC
Chambersburg PA
CBHW021322190726
48288CB00003B/918